MILLIE MAVEN
AND THE GOLDEN VIAL

TED DEKKER & RACHELLE DEKKER

Cover art and design by Manuel Preitano

Printed in the U.S.A.

ISBN 978-1-7335718-4-5

CHAPTER ONE

Approaching the FarPointe Institute for Gifted Students felt like a dream. The stone structure towered three stories into the clear sky. Until today, we'd only seen the institute looming in the distance. The sun was bright; birds sang happy songs; I could feel Mac's and Boomer's excitement. But I was nervous. I'm sure we all were.

Camp was now far behind us. After last night's celebration, we had all awakened to assigned tasks to help tear down and pack up. Once the camp was dismantled, they'd led us up the grassy hill toward FIGS and down a wide gravel road lined with oak trees. A manicured lawn stretched for acres to either side. The road led all the way to the mansion's main entrance. Twelve wide steps made of smooth stone rose to oak doors standing at least fifteen feet high with heavy brass fixtures.

The air was filled with a nervous energy and my head spun with questions. What could be coming next? The three challenges in our Initiation Trial had been frightening—was our journey going to get harder? What would be waiting for us inside the school?

The building looked like an old English countryside mansion of gray brick lined with windows. The institute was shaped like a squared U, each wing topped by a steep shingled roof. I felt overwhelmed moving into its shadow as the Leads took us up the steps.

I wrapped my fingers around the half-dollar-size medallion that hung around my neck. It was cool and smooth against my skin and I took a deep breath. To think only two days earlier I'd been ready to flee FIGS. I hadn't yet met Rebecca or the Great Teacher, and the woodsman hadn't shown his true face. I'd been a slave to the voices of fear that told me I was worthless.

But then I'd surrendered to the truth of the Great Teacher and received the red medallion, and everything had changed. I still heard those voices of self-doubt and felt their sting, but the Great Teacher's assurance called me forward and gave me strength to face those fears.

Riggs pushed open the heavy oak doors and ushered us through. Chaplin brought up the back of the group as we moved into FIGS's main entryway. It was a large half-circle space with white marble floors and high ceilings. A large golden chandelier sparkled from the sun streaming in through the large windows. Fourteen windows in all, I counted, seven across in two rows. I could see the oak trees and perfect lawn through the shimmering glass.

Dean Kyra stood between us and a grand staircase. Six wide wooden steps reached a landing and then split to the right and left, continuing up to the second floor. My gaze followed the wooden railing etched with intricate carvings and supported by thick, twisted iron balusters. The entire room took my breath away. I'd never seen anything like it.

"Welcome, students," Dean Kyra said, drawing my attention back to her. The professors stood to either side, Professors Alexandria and Tomas to her left, Professors Claudia and Gabriel to her right. All wore their navy tunics with matching slacks and black boots, except for Professor Gabriel, who was barefoot. I caught his eye and he winked from behind his wire-rimmed glasses. He made me smile, but I sensed the cold stare of Professor Alexandria lingering on me. She still didn't approve of me being here, because although I'd received a medallion, I didn't yet have a gift.

I swallowed and dropped my eyes. I wouldn't let

her ruin this day. I did belong here. The Great Teacher himself had called me.

"We are so thrilled to have this year's new group of students moving into our grand FarPointe Institute," Dean Kyra said. "Over the next three weeks you will be introduced to an entirely new way of being. Your gifts will be tested, your minds broadened, and your hearts explored."

She paused, looking us over. "Look at the students around you. They are the same as you. Brothers and sisters in this world. You twenty-one are about to embark on a journey very few take. Although it will not be easy, the next trial will unite you and make you stronger than you could have thought possible."

Mac looped her arm through mine, something I was becoming accustomed to her doing. I smiled back at her.

"But with great transformation and change comes great sacrifice," Dean Kyra said in a more serious tone. "Remember, the true power you will learn is that of the heart. Here in the world of FIGS, it will be tested to its core. We hope to see each one of you through to the end, but if at any point you decide you are not ready, you are free to leave and return to where you came from, with no memory of ever being here."

After facing the Initiation Trial, we all knew how serious she was.

"But today you are all here, and that is something to be proud of. I honor each you," she said, holding up her hands toward the wall behind us.

We turned as a group as several banners unfurled one at a time. They hung from gold rope about six feet from the ceiling. The banners were rectangular and three yards long, shimmering silk that blocked some of the high windows and spilled their colors across the marble floor. Each vibrant banner displayed a symbol embroidered with silver thread.

"Blue for our Transformation students, bearing the symbol of the sun as it transforms the winter to spring," Dean Kyra started. "Green for those with Nurturing talents, bearing the symbol of an oak tree, which grows tall and spreads its roots deep beneath the earth."

A third banner fell open in gold and silver. "Metallic shades for gifts of Strength, bearing the symbol of a mountain that stands strong against the changing tides."

"And for the first time," Dean Kyra said and a fourth banner unrolled, "red, the color of the Great Teacher, bearing the symbol of a humble crown for his great sacrifice."

I smiled so wide the corners of my mouth hurt. Mac

squeezed my arm as we stared up at the banners that symbolized what we'd accomplished so far.

"There is so much more to come from each and every one of you," Dean Kyra said, and we turned back to face her. Her eyes were full of pride. "I believe that deeply. But that is for tomorrow. Today you will get settled." She motioned for Riggs and Chaplin to step forward.

"The Leads will show you to your dorms. Take a moment to get familiar with your surroundings. The school is yours, so explore if you'd like. Dinner will be at six o'clock sharp." Again she smiled brightly. "Welcome to you all." She began to clap and the other teachers joined. Within a moment we were all applauding and excited chatter rippled among the students.

"Oh man," Mac said. "I'm so excited I could explode." She bounced in her stance. "What kind of secrets do you think they've got around here?"

"Hopefully the kind that leads us to food," Boomer said. "I'm starving."

Mac rolled her eyes. "How can you even think of food at a time like this?"

Boomer smiled mischievously. "I'm always thinking about food. I've got to feed these muscles."

I laughed, watching Mac fail to suppress a smile.

The soft click of boots sounded behind me, and I turned to see Dean Kyra approaching. She smiled at us and we all stood up straighter.

"Hello," she said. "Millie, will you accompany me for a moment?"

I could feel the other students' curious eyes on me. I nodded and followed.

"Teacher's pet," someone hissed under her breath as I passed by, and heat ran down my spine. I glanced over my shoulder to see Doris Elite staring me down, her twin brother, Dash, at her side. I sent a glare back.

"Jealous much?" Mac teased.

A couple other students snickered and red darkened Doris's cheeks. "I'm not jealous of *her*," Doris bit off.

"Too bad nobody believes you," Mac said.

More snickers. Doris looked like she wanted to rip Mac's head off. She might have if Riggs hadn't interrupted.

"All right, saplings, let's move," he said.

Doris continued to stare. I could feel her hatred cold on my neck as I focused on Dean Kyra. She was observing without a word, and I felt embarrassed.

CHAPTER TWO

I followed Dean Kyra toward a set of double doors along the right side of the foyer. The voices of Riggs and the students diminished as they went the other way.

Dean Kyra pushed open the double doors to reveal a wide hall. It too had marble floors and a high ceiling. The walls were painted a dark maroon, and two smaller brass chandeliers illuminated the space. There were no windows, only a set of double doors on the right wall and three single doors on the left. The farthest door was secured with a thick padlock.

Mac's words filtered through my brain. What kind of secrets *are* they hiding?

"This way," Dean Kyra said, yanking me from my thoughts as she pushed through the double doors. I followed her, chasing away my curiosity, and stepped into a vast library.

"Whoa," I whispered.

"Yes," Dean Kyra responded. "'Whoa' is right."

The room was a huge rectangle. Floor-to-ceiling windows took up the far wall, and sunlight played against every surface. Along the side walls, rows of bookshelves jutted out into the room. A wide aisle cut the center from the double doors to the windows. Collections of small tables and chairs, all white, had been placed along the aisle.

The bookshelves stood twenty to a side, each row fifteen feet high and twice as long. Made of thick oak, the shelves housed books of all different colors and sizes. Hundreds and hundreds of books.

"This is my favorite place in the entire institute," Dean Kyra said. "It was always where you would have found me when I was a student."

I turned to her. "You went to FIGS?"

"Yes, all the professors did. Come, I'll show you."

She walked down the aisle toward the back of the room. My eyes wandered down each row as we passed. I was in awe of how many books could exist in one place. At the last row, Dean Kyra turned left. There, where the left wall met the back corner, was a picture tree of sorts. Plastered against the sturdy wall were hundreds of square photos, some in black and white, others in color. They formed long lines that rose to a triangular point. A banner had been painted on the wall above the photos.

"'Remembering the past to see the future,'" I read out loud. I stepped closer and saw each photo marked with a first name.

Tomlin, a smiling boy with black hair and crooked teeth.

Samantha, with freckled cheeks and blue eyes.

Rachel, in black and white but with bright, kind eyes.

The photos dotted the wall, nearly reaching the ceiling.

"Are these past students?" I asked.

Dean Kyra smiled and pointed to a photo of a small dark-skinned girl with a short black bob and caramel eyes. The photo was marked *Kyra*. I looked up at the dean, unable to keep a smile from my face.

"That was some time ago, before I lost my natural hair color," she teased.

I chuckled. The picture beside the dean's was of a scrawny boy with short brown hair, a missing front tooth, green eyes, and wire-rimmed glasses. The name made me smile. *Gabriel.*

"Is this—"

Dean Kyra started chuckling before I could finish, and her amusement answered my question. "Time has a way of changing us."

"There are so many photos," I said.

"FarPointe Institute has been standing for centuries, long before I was that girl in the photo, and it will continue long after I'm gone." Her eyes lingered on the images.

"But some come back, like you and the Leads. What happens to the others?"

I knew from her expression she wasn't going to give me a straight answer.

"We all take our own journeys, Millie, while in the world of FIGS and after. Your photo will join these, and it will hold a special meaning for me."

"Because of the red medallion?"

She shook her head slightly. "The red medallion is just a symbol. You were given it because of who you are, not the other way around. Please try to remember that."

I smiled and nodded, though I wasn't sure I understood.

"Come," Dean Kyra said. "This is not why I brought you here."

She moved across the room toward the other side, and I saw a locked cabinet tucked in the back corner.

As she made her way there, Dean Kyra reached into her pocket and withdrew a small brass key.

"What's in there?" I asked.

"I keep very little from the students, but there are a couple manuscripts and items that aren't for public display." She popped the key into the lock and gave a small twist. The lock snapped open. She removed it and opened one door.

She bent forward, fumbling around inside as I anxiously waited. When she straightened a few moments later, she was holding a small white book. After closing and re-locking the cabinet, she turned and extended the book to me.

I took it. The soft white leather binding was smooth under my fingertips. It was plain except for a thin sword embossed in the cover's center.

I ran my fingers over the indentation and then opened the cover. The inside was blank, so I flipped through the first few pages. They felt rough and thick between my fingers.

"They're blank," I said.

"There is much mystery surrounding this journal, but the sword on the cover is known as the sword of truth," Dean Kyra said. "The journal has been passed down since the time the Great Teacher himself walked the school grounds, when he held the red medallion."

I turned the book over in my hands as I listened.

"The Great Teacher created all that you see in the world of FIGS, originally known as Eden. He placed this school in its center. He designed the medallions and identified the gifts they represent."

Dean Kyra smiled as her mind captured a memory. "In the beginning the Great Teacher called every student here by name. All who came walked with him, talked with him. They adored him and he loved them fiercely. They say the children wielded limitless power as they sought the Great Teacher with all their hearts."

"What happened?"

"One night a young boy met a hooded man in the woods, and this man started to manipulate the boy's mind. He befriended the boy and sold him lies of glory, reward, security. More children started to listen. More children began to follow the hooded deceiver."

"Soren," I said without needing to be told. I knew him well.

Dean Kyra nodded. "As they listened to Soren's lies, they strayed from the Great Teacher's lessons of love. The farther they strayed, the more afraid they became. Their gifts started to weaken because they were no longer following the Great Teacher."

"What happened to the Great Teacher?"

Dean Kyra's expression became somber. "Those children that he loved so much became so afraid, so convinced by Soren's lies, that they killed the Great Teacher."

"No," I said in shock. "That can't be true."

"Sadly, it is true," Dean Kyra continued. "But that is the power of his story. Because, although no one has seen him since, we know the Great Teacher is very much alive. You are the first child to hear his voice directly since he was betrayed."

"Why me?"

"I do not know. His ways are mysterious but always for our good. Remember, unless a seed falls into the earth and dies, it does not bear fruit."

I wasn't sure I understood what she meant, but she continued before I could ask.

"I want you to have this journal. It belonged to the Great Teacher, and I believe it is meant for you and will guide you."

Millie. Millie, darling, time to come home.

The voice, sticky sweet and forced, flowed like a whisper through my ears. I turned to see who had spoken. The library was still empty except for Dean Kyra and me.

"Are you alright?" Dean Kyra asked.

I turned back and nodded. "I thought I heard something." I looked at the book in my hands. "What am I supposed to do with it?"

"When the student is ready, the teacher will come. You will know when the time is right," Dean Kyra said. "Follow the voice of the Great Teacher. He will never lead you astray."

I opened my mouth to ask her to explain, but the sweet yet terrifying voice floated across my shoulders again.

Millie.

I turned and searched. Was I hearing things? *Millie, darling.*

A figure stood at the other end of the wide aisle. She was plump with poorly dyed blond hair and a face plastered with makeup. A warning bell rang in my head.

"Millie?" Dean Kyra's hand rested on my shoulder. I jumped at her touch, and the library doors burst open. A gaggle of students wandered in, and their excited chatter stole the silence.

The plump woman was gone.

"Millie." Mac's voice reached me. I saw my friend emerge from the gathering. She waved me over, and I shook off the fear that seemed to have rooted my feet.

Dean Kyra released my shoulder. I pulled the journal close to my chest. She looked at it, then at me. "Keep it close," she said.

"I will," I said.

She smiled and nodded toward Mac. "Join your friends. I'll see you later."

Mac was still waving, her eyes excited. She must have discovered something she couldn't wait to tell me. *So have I*, I thought. I stole one more glance at the spot where the plump woman had been and found it empty.

I was hearing and seeing things no one else could. Again.

Great, I thought. *Welcome to FIGS, Millie.*

CHAPTER THREE

"This way, Millie," Mac called.

I rushed after the redhead as she bobbed toward the grand staircase. I'd missed the school tour, and Mac had accepted the challenge of showing me everything she'd discovered.

She skipped the dining hall, located on the first floor, because dinner was in an hour. Instead she headed straight for the stairs, talking the whole time. I excitedly followed her up the left set of steps to the second floor.

"Up the right steps you'll find the boys' dorms and a bunch of teachers' offices."

At the top we stepped into a wide hallway that ended at a brick wall. Three large windows spilled light onto the wood floor. Behind me an identical hallway met the other set of stairs.

"So, boys' dorms are over there?" I asked, pointing. "And the teachers' offices?"

"Yeah," Mac said at my side. "Teachers' offices on the left, dorms on the right."

The crystal chandelier hanging from the high ceiling cast light fragments across the stairs and the foyer below. It was even bigger up close, and although it was still way out of reach, I almost felt like I could touch it.

"Cool, right?" Mac said.

I nodded and turned back to the girls' hall. To the right was a line of doors.

"What's there?" I tipped my chin toward them.

"A common area," Mac answered. "There's a larger one downstairs that's tricked out with cool stuff. I'll show you before dinner. This one up here is simpler, more for studying. It holds memorabilia from the school's history—there's an entire display of old weapons they used to train with. Secured behind glass of course. It's pretty cool. Beside that"—she pointed—"two lecture halls, A and B. That's where we'll have classes."

"What kind of classes?"

"This is why we're friends! I asked the same question."

I smiled at her dramatic flair.

"According to Riggs, the classes are simple. History of gifts and the institute. Learning how to call upon gifts and control them. Things like that. But he made a point of saying most of our learning won't happen in there."

"Where will it happen?" I asked.

"Asked that too, and he wouldn't answer. He just did one of those sneaky smiles, like he has a secret. You know what I'm talking about?"

I did. Sneaky smiles seemed to be a required skill for all who worked at FIGS.

"Come on," Mac said. She started down the hall and I followed.

"I thought there was a third floor. Did you guys get to see that?" I asked.

"There is, and no. That's where the professors and Dean Kyra live. We were kindly asked not to wander around up there." Mac paused and checked to make sure we were alone. Then she gave me her own sneaky smile. "Which means I totally want to. Is that terrible?"

I giggled at her wide eyes and she shook her head. "I'm just so curious is all," she said innocently. She turned down a narrower hall to our left. It also ran to a bricked end, but this one had only a single window. Two doors sat directly across from one another on either side of the hallway. Three brass light fixtures in the ceiling gave off warm yellow light.

"These are the girls' dorms," Mac said.

She led me to the door on the right and grabbed the thick brass knob. "They separated us into two groups, five in this room and five in the other. You're in here with me."

A thrill buzzed in my chest. "I'm glad they didn't split us up," I admitted.

"No way," Mac said. "We're in this together, no matter what."

"No matter what," I confirmed. And I sensed in that moment, even without my memories, that I'd never had a friendship so strong.

Mac twisted the knob and pushed open our dorm door. We walked inside and my heart soared. The room was a long rectangle with light blue walls and a white painted ceiling. A small brass chandelier decorated with little crystal teardrops hung above the center. The longest wall, directly across from the entry, housed five white-framed windows. Two more were in the wall to my left. To the right, the word *Bathroom* had been painted in black cursive letters over another door.

Eight single canopy beds made of dark wood, four on each side, were draped with gauzy white material.

In the center of the room, three lavender chairs sat around a coffee table on a violet rug. Behind me, four tall dressers flanked the doorway, two on each side. A wall clock hung above the door.

Mac grabbed my hand and gently pulled me toward two beds in the corner.

"I claimed these for us," she said, releasing my hand and plopping down on the one against the wall. I sat on the one she'd saved for me and sank into the thick mattress. I ran my hand across the soft and smooth comforter. All the beds were accented with different-colored blankets. Mine yellow and Mac's green.

Each bed had a small bedside table and a trunk at the foot. A large vanity with a round mirror sat near the bathroom door, a waist-high bookshelf stood along the long wall, and three more chairs with dark blue cushions had been tucked into corners.

The space was beautiful. A sense of comfort settled into my bones. Mac exhaled and fell back against her bed. I followed suit, placing my head on the pillow. For a long moment we laid in silence, each lost in our own thoughts.

"I don't spend a lot of time thinking about what my life was like before coming here," Mac said. "Not because I'm not curious, because we both know that

I am, but because being here is such an adventure. I don't want to miss anything by getting stuck in what came before."

She went quiet for a second. "But having a room like this makes me wonder what my room was like before. Could it have been this grand? Did I feel this good being there? Did I share it with a sister maybe?"

She rolled onto her side and I did the same so that we were facing one another. "Do you ever miss home?" she asked.

I thought about her question and searched my heart. "I don't know. When I think about it, I mostly feel afraid, and I think maybe the place I came from wasn't really home. Not like this."

"What do you think will happen when we have to leave?" Mac asked.

"I don't want to think about having to leave this place," I answered, feeling my chest fill with emotion. "Or you."

"You know I get feelings about things, like I knew you were going to be special. And I just get the feeling that we are meant to be friends forever."

I smiled. "Me too."

A soft chime sounded from a distance, and Mac shot up, glancing at the wall clock. Nearly six.

Time for dinner.

"We gotta go," she said, sweeping her feet around and off her bed.

CHAPTER FOUR

The dining hall, like everything else at FIGS, was grand. Light-wood panels covered the floor and the ceiling towered twenty feet overhead. A dozen bright round light fixtures doused the room in warm light. Twelve white-top round tables sat six people each. And down the center of the room was a bulky wooden table holding a feast.

The impressive array was a marvel. I hadn't realized how hungry I was until I saw the hot food: fried chicken, meatloaf, spaghetti, steak, turkey legs, mashed potatoes, yams, corn, green beans, asparagus, cranberries, strawberries, fresh peaches, apples, rice, sweet rolls, garlic bread, salad with a dozen dressing options, and more.

We devoured the spread like hungry orphans, most going back for seconds. Our chatter filled the room. When we had our fill, a team of kitchen attendants dressed in white quickly replaced the feast with a dessert buffet. I thought Boomer was going to pass out from excitement. Mac and I laughed at his enthusiasm.

I wasn't sure I could eat another bite, but there was no way I was passing up the warm chocolate cake. Each mouthful smelled and tasted like heaven. When I cleaned my plate, I was certain Mac and Boomer were going to have to roll me back to the dorms.

We were dismissed with instructions to be back in our dorms by eight. Mac and I walked with Boomer and his bunkmate, Harvey Lector, toward the first-floor common area. I'd seen Harvey around. He was a tall thin kid with shaggy blond hair and piercing blue eyes. He didn't speak much, but when he did it was clear he was very smart.

The common area sat behind the grand staircase. Mac had been right: it was fully tricked out. It had soft blue carpet, light bricked walls, and oddities I hadn't expected.

A pool table and a foosball table sat to the left, with colorful couches on both walls for spectators. An art station with several art easels and baskets of supplies occupied one corner.

To the right was an old pinball machine and a gathering of bright beanbags as well as more couches, one striped orange and white, another topped with yellow pillows. In the right corner a worktable had been placed beside a large bookshelf stuffed with comics, magazines, and books.

But the grandest thing of all was the huge brick fireplace in the center of the back wall. I could stand inside of it and stretch my arms in both directions without touching the sides.

Mac pulled me over to the comfy couches and we settled in. We sat there for a while swapping stories from the day and laughing at Boomer's antics. Harvey didn't say a word as Boomer did all the talking.

He told us about the boys' dorms. They had bunkbeds rather than singles, five boys in one room and six in the other.

"Honestly, I'm glad they split us up," Boomer said, then leaned in slightly and dropped his voice. "There are certain people I'd rather not have to see." He gave a *you know what I mean* look, and it was clear we all did. The room was filling with more students, little groups taking up different corners.

"I'm not even sure I'd feel safe sleeping," Boomer continued. "I mean, who knows what could be done to me? That's why Harvey and I made a pact to protect each other."

Boomer looked at the lengthy boy. "I've got his back and he's got mine. Isn't that right, Harv?"

Harvey nodded and Boomer returned the gesture, seemingly satisfied. Mac's mouth was turning up in a smirk but fell straight as her eyes caught sight of something.

"Speak of the devil," she whispered, and the rest of us followed her gaze. Dash and Doris entered and without missing a beat beelined right for us, the Elite lackeys in tow. The twins never seemed to go anywhere without their entourage.

Maverick: a handsome boy with dark hair and eyes, nearly as tall as Dash, but broader through the shoulders. Adam: a quick, sneaky boy, smaller than Maverick, and constantly wearing a mischievous expression. Sid: who looked like he wouldn't mind getting his hands dirty if instructed. Ciara: a dark-skinned girl with beautiful curly hair and a sinister gaze. And Gwendolyn: a striking blond who caught the attention of every boy but looked at them as if they were dirt.

They passed through the room like a plague. The other students inched back to avoid being infected. This gang always brought trouble with them. I was tiring of it.

"Misfit Millie and her mangey crew," Dash said, and without missing a beat Doris finished his thought.

"Still pretending to be worthy of being here?"

Their creepy twin thing made me squirm.

"Still pretending we care what you think?" Mac fired back. We all wanted not to care, but I saw the flicker of fear that flashed across Boomer's face. It was the same kind that spiked in my belly. These bullies were bigger, meaner, more vocal. I just wanted them to pick on someone else.

"Are you always going to let Mackenzie fight your battles for you, Millie Maven?" Doris asked.

Mac stood and opened her mouth to fire back. I grabbed her wrist as I stood. "Don't," I said. "It's not worth it. Let's just go."

Doris huffed. "That's right, Misfit Millie, run away like you do."

I ignored her baiting and—with Mac, Boomer, and Harvey in tow—walked out.

"Might as well leave now," Doris tossed at me.

I could feel my anger slowing my pace.

"No one wants you here anyway," she said.

I stopped and turned back to face her, feeling the eyes of the room.

"That isn't true," I said.

Doris stepped toward me. "A girl without a gift at a school for the gifted. What are you even doing here?"

"I was called here."

Doris laughed. "Called?"

"By the Great Teacher," I said, finding strength in my words. She opened her mouth to rebut, but I cut her off. I reached for the medallion around my neck and pulled it free. "He gave me this, his medallion, the only one of its kind."

The mockery in her eyes had started to fade because she knew I was right. I could have left it at that and walked away, but my anger was strong, and I was tired of her thinking she could prod at me whenever she wanted. So I threw a final punch.

"What did he give you?" Even as the words came out of my mouth I knew they didn't sound like me. I ignored the soft warning in my heart and felt the rush of strength that came from silencing my enemy.

As I turned to leave I heard Doris's low and cruel voice.

"You'll regret this, Millie Maven."

I didn't answer. My strength was already fading back to fear.

CHAPTER FIVE

Mac and I said good night to the boys and headed back to our dorm. We hung out for half an hour alone, then the other girls in our room joined us.

Lianna: a mousey girl with dirt-brown hair and dark eyes. Polly: tall and thin with black hair, the ends dyed hot pink. And Olive: a beautiful blond with light-green eyes and perfect teeth. I was relieved our dorm was Elite-lackey-free. It made me feel safe. It also meant that Doris, Ciara, and Gwendolyn were just across the hall together, where they could plot my doom.

Collene was in there with them and a girl I didn't know well named Amanda. Collene had always been nice to me. Maybe she'd give me a heads-up if she heard something dastardly being planned. My bunkmates didn't say much when they entered, followed by Chaplin.

"You should find everything you need for bed in your trunks and bathroom," Chaplin said, standing inside the door. "Lights out in twenty. I'll be back then." She pulled the door closed as she left.

We all moved around silently, finding sleepwear and using the bathroom. The air felt tense, though I couldn't put my finger on why. Olive and I were the last to brush our teeth. The bathroom had two large pedestal sinks, a tiled shower tucked around the corner, and a toilet stall. It was simple and clean, everything white.

I turned off the water and placed my toothbrush in a holder marked with my initials hanging on the wall. I caught Olive's glance in the large rectangular mirror that hung over both sinks.

I offered a smile and she returned it.

"Doris is a bully," Olive said. "I'm sorry she's always coming after you."

Her kind words struck me. I hadn't expected them. Olive left the small tiled room and I followed. Lianna was already sitting in bed, her legs tucked under blankets. She'd chosen the empty bed beside mine.

Polly was standing beside her chosen bed next to Olive's. They were across the room from Lianna, Mac, and me.

"I'm glad you stood up to Doris tonight," Polly said as I walked toward my bed.

Mac was dressed in white pajamas and sat cross-legged in one of the purple chairs to my right. Had they been talking about what happened?

"Someone needed too," Polly continued.

I felt a bit self-conscious with them all looking at me and hoped my face wasn't flush. "Thanks," I said. "I probably shouldn't have."

"Why not?" Olive asked, moving to sit on her bed beside Polly's. "She can't just get away with talking to you like that."

The room went quiet for a moment.

"I bet it felt good," Polly said. "For a moment she looked scared of you."

"Yeah, and she sulked after you left," Olive said.

"Good," Mac said. "Maybe she'll back off now."

I wanted Mac to be right, but I knew Doris wasn't one for backing down.

"We should make a pact," Mac said. We all looked to her. "We're roommates now, so we need to have each other's backs. Like Dean Kyra said. Sisters."

Mac stood and moved to the center of the room beside me. She reached out her hand for me to take, and I clasped it. Then Mac offered her free hand toward Polly. Both she and Olive moved to join, Polly grasping Mac's hand and offering hers to Olive. A near circle, I extended my hand back toward the small Lianna, who still hadn't spoken. She smiled, climbed out of bed, and joined us.

"No matter what," Mac started. "We are together. We protect each other. We'll be stronger together."

"Together," Polly said.

"Together," the rest of us joined, even Lianna.

"And if we need to, we kick Doris's butt," Lianna said softly.

She caught us all off guard and we started giggling. It felt good for a moment but I also felt a warning somewhere deep. I tossed it aside for the comaradery and smiled with my friends.

The door popped open and Chaplin stuck her head in. "Lights out, girls."

We disbanded, each girl taking her bed, and shared knowing looks before tucking ourselves in.

"If you need anything, I'm in the room near the end of the hall," Chaplin said. "See you in the morning." With that the lights went out and the door shut.

"Night, Millie," Mac whispered.

"Night," I replied. I was afraid the excitement of the day would keep me wired, but sleep took me in minutes. And in that sleep, a dream swallowed me whole.

Not just any dream. In fact, maybe it wasn't a dream

at all, because it felt far more real than any dream I could remember. One moment I was nowhere, and the next I was standing among fiery torches affixed to stone walls in an otherwise dark cavern.

I looked around and saw I was in a cave with a clear pool that reflected the flames on the walls.

My brain buzzed. I had been here before. "Once through the water, time changes," a voice said.

I turned toward it and gasped. An older woman with short white hair and blue eyes was speaking to a young girl. The girl was me. Neither one seemed to notice I was there.

"One day there might be a week beyond the pool, so you'll have plenty of time," the kind woman said. "There's nothing to fear. Nothing here, that is." The entire scene was so familiar.

Had I lived this?

With that question, I knew where I was. This was Aggie talking to me before I'd gone through the pool to FIGS. It was a memory.

But it couldn't be! I wasn't supposed to remember anything. Maybe I was wrong and this was just a dream, but I doubted it. I could remember clearly now.

"Hello," I said to myself and the woman. "Can you see me?"

They didn't respond or react. I was invisible. The realization sent a chill down my spine.

The twin me spoke, clearly nervous. "A week? How would I even know when to come back?"

"Well, these things aren't precise, but if you insist on being back before sunrise . . ."

Sunrise? The old woman went on but I was distracted by that word. Aggie was trying to comfort the girl . . . well, comfort me, who was the girl. Something about sunrise was very important to her. To me.

Another voice cut through the cavern. "Millie."

I froze because this voice was airy and chilling.

"Do you really think you can defy me, darling?" But there was nothing darling about the sound of the voice. It so disturbed me that I dared not turn around.

Aggie was talking: "Five days then." She was telling me to return within five days to be safe. It was the last I heard before the sinister voice behind me spoke again.

"You will regret this, Millie," it snapped. "How dare you defy me!"

I was afraid to turn, but then I was turning. There stood a woman glaring at me with harsh black eyes. She was plump with blond hair, caked-on makeup, and dark eyeshadow, and was standing against the cave's back wall.

Terror crawled into my skin. I stood frozen.

A hand touched my shoulder and yanked me from the terrifying woman's gaze. I whipped around to see the old woman had gone. Only my twin was there now. But I looked different: my face gray, dark circles under my drained eyes, my skin pulled tight across my bones.

"Tick, tock," the twisted version of me said. "The sun is rising."

I let out a scream that echoed through the cave and rocked me awake.

I shot up in bed, my heart thundering against my ribs. My breath was short as my senses started to take over. I was in bed, back in the dorm, the room dark with night and silent except for the other girls' breathing. And my racing pulse.

The clock over the door blinked the time: 1:15 a.m.

I'd been dreaming. But I knew it was more. I remembered something. I remembered Aggie, the pool, coming through. I remembered she told me I had to get back before sunrise or I'd be in terrible trouble. In trouble with the terrifying woman in the cave. The same one I'd seen in the library.

How dare you defy me?

A shiver raked my spine because I knew I would suffer dreadful punishment if I defied her. I wasn't sure who she was, but she was real and I had to get back before she knew I was gone!

I yanked the covers back and threw my legs from the bed. Careful not to wake anyone, I moved to the door and quietly opened it. I slipped into the hallway and shut the door softly. My heart rammed.

Okay, think, Millie. It couldn't be a memory; that wasn't supposed to happen. But I knew too many specifics for it to be anything else. And my body knew the memory. I had lived it, and the message was clear.

The sun was rising wherever I had come from, and if I didn't get back . . .

It was enough to spur me into action. I rushed down the hall toward the main staircase. I considered backtracking to Chaplin's room, but I hadn't spent much time with the Lead and I wasn't sure how she'd react. But at this time of night, I wasn't sure who else I expected to find.

I reached the banister and looked down. The main floor was dark and quiet. Across the grand stairway, the wing to the boys' dorms was much the same, except for a light glow coming from under a closed door.

Teachers' offices. Someone was awake. Or had left the light on. I couldn't be sure without checking. What if it was Professor Alexandria? I might be better to try my chances with Chaplin. But it could just as easily be Dean Kyra or Professor Gabriel. Right?

I silenced my worry and walked around the

curved banister toward the light. Swallowing my fear, I approached the door and twisted the knob without knocking. I stepped into the lit space and saw a white-haired man sitting at a wide oak desk.

Relief flooded my senses. Professor Gabriel, unstartled, gave me a curious look. "Miss Maven? What are you doing out of bed?"

When I saw the comforting ally, full panic rushed over my body. I walked into the room, not bothering to shut the door. "I . . . I think . . ." I couldn't get the words out.

Professor Gabriel stood and crossed the room toward me. "It's alright, child." He placed his hand on my shoulder and led me to a cushioned chair in the corner. He motioned for me to sit. I did, trying to get my heart back to a normal rhythm. He took an identical chair on the other side of a small table.

"Did you have a nightmare?"

I shook my head no. "I had a memory."

"A memory?" he asked.

"From my life before. It was awful, and I remembered that I can't be here anymore. I have to get back or I'll be in terrible trouble."

"How do you know it was a memory and not simply a dream?"

I looked up at him. "I just know. I saw myself there

at the pool with Aggie, the woman who sent me here. I know it was real." I could feel myself on the verge of tears.

"Oh, Professor Gabriel, I have to get back. I have to."

"There, there, Millie. It's alright. You're alright," Professor Gabriel said, patting my shoulder.

"I'm not alright. You have no idea the trouble I'm facing. They are monsters."

"Monsters? No, honey, surely they are just people."

"Not her, not the one I saw in the library."

"Who did you see in the library?" he asked, his voice calm and warm.

I searched my mind but couldn't find her name. I only remembered the fear that raged in my gut when I saw her. But then, I'd also been terrified when I saw myself, and I wasn't a monster. Was I? No, of course not.

Professor Gabriel took my silence as an answer. "Have you considered perhaps your mind is playing tricks on you?"

I had considered maybe it was just a dream. But it felt so real.

As if reading my thoughts, the teacher continued: "The mind can be a tricky thing, Millie. And after all you have faced this last week, it would make sense that your mind might be processing it in unusual ways."

I sniffed back the tears that blurred my vision.

"It was so real, Professor Gabriel."

"Yes, when in a dream it can feel as real as being awake. Can I share a secret with you?" His eyes sparkled and I nodded.

"I sometimes have food dreams," he said.

"What's that?"

"Simple as it sounds: I dream of food. And I swear I can taste the food on my tongue, yet when I wake up, I am in my bed, no food to be seen."

I gave a weak smile, my heart slowing. "Really?"

"Yes. I wake starving."

My smile grew. "So you think it was just a dream, and I'm not in terrible trouble?"

"You are safe at FIGS, discovering who you are," Professor Gabriel said. "The Great Teacher is with you, so what do you have to fear?"

So quickly I'd forgotten the words of the Great Teacher. So easily I'd given in to my fears. He'd told me he was always with me, which meant even now. I took a deep breath. It must have just been a nightmare. I suddenly felt a little silly for panicking.

Again Professor Gabriel must have read my expression. He gave my shoulder a squeeze. "We all succumb to the madness of fear."

"Even you?" I asked.

He chuckled. "Of course!"

"What do you do then?"

"I focus on something greater than fear. Love. The love the Great Teacher has for me and all the world. A love that casts out fear. It gives me strength. It will give you strength too."

Yes, I thought. *I have felt the love of the Great Teacher.* I smiled, feeling much better and very tired.

"Would you like me to walk you back to your dorm room?" Professor Gabriel asked.

I nodded and we stood. He escorted me back through the silent school, and with each step I started to feel more certain it had only been a dream. When we reached the narrow hallway, he paused and placed his hand on my shoulder once more.

"Sleep well, Miss Maven. May your dreams bring you peace."

"Thank you, Professor Gabriel," I said.

"That's what I'm here for, dear." He watched as I walked the hall to my dorm and gave a small wave once I reached it. Back inside I snuck to bed, crawled in, and quickly fell asleep. Peacefully.

CHAPTER SIX

Priscilla Pruitt woke up and went about her morning as usual. A warm bath to start, the water soaking her dry, wrinkled skin. Vanilla body lotion from neck to toes, the smell infecting her entire bathroom. A white silk top with matching cotton trousers, pearls around her neck, diamond studs in her ears.

Heavy foundation, white powder, dark-pink blush, and violet eyeshadow. A shade lighter than usual, but she was wearing white, so it suited the look. Last, black kitten heels, her favorite pair.

She stepped back to admire herself in the floor-length mirror inside her bedroom. The buttons at the top of her blouse pulled a tad across her chest and she huffed, annoyed. This was Millie's fault. She'd forced Priscilla to break her diet and eat the birthday cupcake the night before.

It had been a necessary action to help the poor girl learn to be better. Discipline needed to be harsh. Memorable. It was for the child's own good. Priscilla wouldn't have a disobedient wretch as a daughter. No, that wouldn't do.

Priscilla believed children could be a gift to the world if they behaved properly. Most did not. Most had lazy parents who'd long forgotten a strict hand was the best way to show love. Spoil a child with too much care and they become entitled.

Priscilla once dreamed of having lots of well-behaved children. When she discovered her body was unable to carry a child, the bitterness of loss had threatened to ruin her entire life. So when the opportunity arose to take in Millie, Priscilla knew it was her chance to have the life she'd dreamed of.

Millie clearly didn't understand the gift she'd been given. If the child had been raised by her birth parents, she'd have turned out to be a stain on society, like so many others.

Priscilla swallowed the dark memories that rose in her when she let herself think of Millie's birth mother, her younger sister, Becky. Pretty, kind, popular, smart, Becky had always been their mother's favorite.

Their father died the day after Priscilla's tenth birthday. Their mother was crushed, broken, and angry. She turned to Priscilla for support while simultaneously blaming her for everything that went wrong.

Becky was only five then, the picture of innocence. Their mother held tightly to this image. No matter what Priscilla did, it was never enough, while sweet little Becky was perfect. Hatred for her lazy younger sibling grew steadily as they aged.

Priscilla worked her way through homeschool classes while tending to their mother and home. Becky begged to go to a real high school and Mother had agreed, a luxury stolen from Priscilla.

During Becky's senior year she met a boy and they fell madly in love. After graduating, Becky got married and abandoned Priscilla with their mother as she and her new husband traveled west for their dreams.

Their mother grew crueler in her old age and died from a heart attack ten years after Becky left home. Priscilla was free but alone. She wasn't good alone. So she'd hitched her wagon to the rich bachelor Augustus Pruitt.

After three years of failed pregnancies, she came into possession of Millie. For the first time in her life, Priscilla felt whole. Nothing would ever separate her from her daughter. Not as long as she was alive.

She adjusted her top, reexamined her appearance, and left her bedroom. Augustus had his own room across the hall. They both enjoyed separate space. His door was open. He was already up and downstairs.

Priscilla descended the staircase. At the bottom of the steps she turned into the large dining room. Breakfast had been laid out for her with the morning newspaper.

She shivered a tad and thought the room felt colder than it should. Her eye caught the fireplace, where the ashes from last night sat gray and dead. *Strange*, she thought. *Millie knows to be up early enough to light the fires on winter days.*

A warning bell chimed in her mind. She couldn't remember a time when Millie had forgotten such a chore.

"Good morning, Mrs. Pruitt," Martha said, entering the room with hot coffee.

"Have you seen Millie yet this morning?" Priscilla asked.

"No, I haven't," Martha said.

The warning grew and Priscilla exhaled her anxiety. It wasn't good to overreact.

"Get her now," Priscilla ordered.

Martha nodded and left. Priscilla felt frustration slither up her back. She would have thought the girl would be on her best behavior after last night's punishment. Clearly Priscilla was being too lenient. The plump woman grabbed the mug on the table and walked to the window.

The ground was covered in snow sparkling like diamonds. Considering the ways she would deal with the child calmed her. She sipped her coffee, eyes wandering, then stopped cold.

There were prints in the snow. Tracks from the house heading west to the edge of the property. They looked like boot tracks. *Impossible*, Priscilla thought.

A terrifying idea popped into her head.

She rushed from the dining room and toward the back of the house, through the kitchen, where Martha's daughter, Abby, was cleaning, and out the back door. Bitter cold air nipped through her silk shirt as Priscilla turned the corner and stopped at the row of tracks.

Definitely boots. Too small to belong to Roger, the property manager. Priscilla stood in shock a long moment before going back into the kitchen.

She stormed to Abby. "Did you go outside this morning?" she demanded.

Abby looked taken aback and stumbled over her words.

"Did you go outside this morning?! Answer me!"

"No, Mrs. Pruitt," Abby said.

"When was the last time you went west of the property?"

"I . . . I can't remember. A couple days at least."

Dread dropped into Priscilla's gut. The only other person with feet that small . . .

Panic yanked her from the kitchen. Snow fell from her shoes as Martha came down the stairs, a worried look in her eyes.

"Finally up," Augustus said to Priscilla's right. He was walking from one of the reading rooms, mug and newspaper in hand. He had returned from China yesterday but still wore his three-piece suit and navy tie. Graying and wrinkled, he looked older than his forty-nine years.

He glanced from Priscilla to Martha and then back to his wife.

"What's wrong?" he asked, voice less than concerned.

Priscilla looked to Martha, hoping for impossible news. Martha hesitated, and Priscilla could feel her husband's concern spark.

"Well?" he demanded.

"She's not in her room," Martha said, barely above a whisper.

"Who's not in her room?" Augustus asked.

Priscilla ignored her husband's questions. "Search everywhere."

The old woman nodded and dashed off.

"What is going on?" Augustus asked.

Priscilla inhaled and turned toward her husband. "Nothing I can't handle. Don't worry."

"I am worried." He took a step forward. "Where is your pet?"

"She is misplaced," Priscilla said.

"Children are not misplaced. They go missing." His voice was low and angry.

Priscilla swallowed. "I will find her."

"How could you have let this happen?"

"She is here somewhere! She wouldn't dare go beyond the fence."

Priscilla opted not to tell him about the tracks in the snow. Not until she knew for certain what she feared.

"And if she did, do you have any idea the danger she could bring us?" Augustus sneered. "Or have you forgotten what you did?"

"I will find her, darlin—"

Augustus hurled his empty mug across the room, where it collided with the wall and smashed into dozens of pieces. He huffed and leaned toward Priscilla's face.

His breath was hot and smelled of black coffee. "I will not lose everything I have built over a worthless orphan."

Then he stepped back, exhaled, ran his fingers through his hair, and threw her one last hateful glare. "Find her!"

The click of Augustus's shoes faded.

She would find the child.

Then she would make sure Millie was severely punished.

CHAPTER SEVEN

I slept soundly the rest of the night, thankful for Professor Gabriel's reassurance. The day started at 8:00 a.m. sharp with clear instructions: we were to ready ourselves, enjoy some breakfast, and be in lecture hall A by 9:30 a.m., not a minute after.

Breakfast was set up like dinner. The array of morning consumptions would satisfy any craving. I scarfed down pancakes, bacon, and several tall glasses of milk before walking to the lecture hall with my dorm girls.

After last night's pact, our room was filled with a new sense of unity. It made me happy but also created a division between us and the other girls. I couldn't stop thinking about how Dean Kyra said we were all connected, all sisters. Yet during breakfast my dorm mates and I had sat at one table while Doris and her dorm mates ate at another.

Doris brought this on herself, I thought. *Because she's mean. A bully.* The justification soothed me and I tossed out any worry as I followed Mac into lecture hall A. I hadn't seen it yet, and I gasped as I entered.

The room was nearly as large as the library, a square with brick walls that stretched to a plain white ceiling. In the center a massive iron chandelier was lit with burning candles instead of lightbulbs.

At the front of the classroom, a heavy wooden desk faced the room. Behind it a wall of shelves held books, candlesticks, small iron chests, and other items I didn't recognize. Sharply ascending rows of bench seats divided by a center aisle took up the back. I counted twenty-five rows, each one capable of seating a dozen students.

Between the desk and the seats was a wide-open space large enough for a group ten times our size.

"Whoa," I whispered.

"I know," Mac responded. "Chaplin told us the walls used to be wood, but they covered them in brick so they wouldn't have to repair them anymore."

"Repair them from what?" I asked.

"Practicing gifts," Mac said.

"You think we'll get to practice using our gifts?" Olive asked.

"What else would we be doing here?" Polly said. "I mean, they have to show us how to use them, right?"

"Please, everyone, come in and find a seat," came a familiar voice from the front of class. Professor Claudia stood dressed in her navy uniform, her gray hair pulled into a tight bun atop her head. Beside her, Professor Tomas watched as we funneled into the room. "Quickly now," Professor Claudia said.

We took to the rows in groups. Mac and I sat with Boomer and Harvey in the fifth row, Polly, Olive, and Lianna joining us. I ended up next to the center aisle.

I could feel hot eyes on my neck and turned slightly to see Doris, Dash, and the Elite lackeys sitting two rows back on the opposite side of the aisle. Doris and I held each other's gaze for a quick moment before something shifted in the corner behind her, drawing my attention.

For a moment I thought I saw the cruel woman from my past. The one from my dream who called me *darling* in a way that made my skin crawl. I let out a soft gasp, then the sight disappeared. Or maybe it hadn't even been there.

"What?" Mac asked.

I turned back to her. "Huh?"

"You gasped; are you okay?"

I exhaled and smiled. "Yeah, just this place is—"

"Awesomesauce."

I giggled and shook my head. She always made me feel better.

"Settle down, students," Professor Tomas said. "Settle."

The class calmed and focused on the instructors.

Professor Claudia smiled brightly. "Welcome to Practical Use of Gifts. Professor Tomas and I are thrilled to finally have you here as we begin the study of our gifts and abilities."

She started to pace. "It is not always the case, but this group represents all the gifts and abilities given by the Great Teacher. This delights me, because it means we have so much goodness to learn."

Professor Tomas spoke up. "I'm sure you have been talking among yourselves about your gifts and what they can do, but let's review."

He stepped into the center of the room and began. "There are three kinds of gifts: Strength, Transformation, and Nurture. Within each gift there are two abilities. Strength gifts either appear in brute strength, commonly called Meats, or—" He disappeared and a gust of wind whipped down the middle aisle, across the back of the room, and returned to the front as quickly as I could snap my fingers. Professor Tomas reappeared before us. "—Quicks, known for their speed," he said.

I smiled at Mac as her eyes widened. The room whispered their excitement as Professor Claudia continued.

"Those with Transformation gifts can appear as Shifters, meaning they have the ability to change the form of a thing into another form of itself, for example, water to ice—" The teacher kindly motioned to Doris, who had done just that during the first trial. "—or Benders."

Professor Claudia went silent for a moment and stared at us intensely. Students around me started to giggle. Then laugh. I found myself amused by something I couldn't understand, and before I knew it, we were all dying of laughter.

Professor Claudia smiled and the laughter died down. "Benders can affect the emotions of another."

She had done that to us? Yes, she'd made us think something was hilarious when nothing was. My mouth opened in wonder. A chill sat on my skin and I felt eyes watching me from the front corner of the class-room. I glanced up and froze. Again the woman from my nightmare appeared to me, silent and still. Staring at me. I blinked hard, and when I opened my eyes she was gone.

I swallowed. My mind was playing cruel tricks on me. That was all.

"Finally," Professor Tomas said. "Nurture gifts display as Healers, who do exactly what the name suggests, or Earthers, such as Dean Kyra, who can manipulate the natural world."

"You might think one gift is more important than another," Professor Claudia said. "But it is crucial to remember that each gift is an expression of the Great Teacher's love. Together they serve the good of all the world. As we teach you about your gifts, the greater lesson will be about your hearts."

Professor Tomas nodded. "It is tempting to believe these displays of wonder are powerful in themselves, but as Dean Kyra has said, the true power comes from your heart. Remember this. Until you learn it, you limit your own strength."

"But don't worry," Professor Claudia said. "We will teach you all we can and give you many opportunities to learn for yourselves."

"What if you don't have a gift?" the hateful voice of Doris barked from behind me. I could feel many eyes and hear the soft snickering of the Elite group.

Professor Tomas and Professor Claudia shared a brief look and I knew they weren't sure what to say. I wanted to melt into the floor. Doris was right. I didn't have a gift like the rest. What was I supposed to do while they trained?

I might have gotten stuck in a mental loop of anxiety if the chilling feeling of being watched hadn't returned. I didn't want to look; I knew what I would find. But an invisible force pulled at me and I couldn't help it. Raising my eyes, I saw her. Same as before.

Still like stone.

Watching me with dark eyes.

Like a tidal wave, all my memories crashed through me. The mansion in Paradise, Colorado. My endless days of chores. My mistakes and punishments. My attic bedroom. The rules that were never to be broken. Hateful Mr. Pruitt.

My mother. The woman standing before me was my mother.

I jumped from my seat. Everyone turned to watch me, but I didn't care. Someone was speaking, but I blocked the voice. Terror poured over me like hot coals. Panic rattled my bones and quickened my breath.

All I could hear were the memories. All I could see was my mother, and I knew I had to get back. Aggie had said I had five days till sunrise. My brain scrambled to count. Was today the fifth day or sixth day? I was out of time. In my head I heard the sticky-sweet voice that filled me with fear.

How dare you leave me!

Tick, tock.

"Miss Maven." Professor Claudia was taking concerned steps toward me. I barely heard her through the chaos in my brain, and what I heard I ignored. Stepping into the center aisle, I rushed down the steps to the main floor. I ran across the room and out the door toward the grand staircase.

Shouts of my name followed me. I kept running down the stairs as quickly as I could. I had to get back before Mother discovered I was gone. I might already be too late! I skipped the last step and raced toward the exit.

My mind tumbled over itself. I remembered that when students chose to leave they were escorted back to the ocean. That must be the way back. Through the water of the sea. Outside, the warm morning touched my skin. I flew down the stone steps and onto the gravel path shaded by the oak trees.

Threatening words and warning bells rang in my ears.

Tick, tock, Millie.

I had forgotten. I had let myself get carried away

with this world of FIGS and forgotten the danger. If Mother caught me gone . . .

I was too afraid to think about what she might do to me.

I came to the end of the gravel road, my chest burning, and stumbled onto the grassy path leading toward the forest.

Now, Millie! The voice rasped from the woods. *Come home now!*

I tripped, fell forward hard, slammed my palms into the dirt, and cried out. I pushed myself up and glanced back. FIGS was gone. This caused me to pause. The solid structure that I'd been in only minutes ago had vanished.

I stood, sadness creeping into my heart. I hadn't said good-bye. Tears sprang to my eyes. I couldn't think about that. I had to get back. I turned back toward the woods just as someone appeared from behind the invisible wall that hid FIGS.

"Millie," he said.

I started walking. "I'm sorry, Professor Gabriel, but I have to go."

"Please, Millie, stop for a moment."

"I can't! It's been five days. Mother will know I'm gone. I can't!"

"I want to understand—"

I whipped around, tears inching down my cheeks. "I remember. I remember everything. My old life, how I got here, how I have to get back. You can't understand."

Tick, tock, Millie.

Better get home.

"More dreams?" he asked.

"They aren't dreams! They are reminders of who I really am back home and how much trouble I'll be in for leaving. *That* is my real life. Is this even real?"

"I assure you this is as real as that. And the lessons you learn here, the power you gain—you will take those with you back to that life."

I wanted to believe him, but my fear was greater than my faith in what he said.

"I should have never come here," I said.

"But you had to come, Millie," Professor Gabriel said softly. "The Great Teacher called you."

"But Aggie said I had to be back!"

"The woman who led you to the pool. Are you sure that's what she said?"

I considered his question. What had she said exactly?

"I don't know this Aggie, but in all my years I've never known a guide to insist a child must return before their training was complete. Did she insist?"

No, I thought. Maybe I had done that. Maybe she was only offering me reassurances. But that didn't make what she said untrue.

"Is time still passing there?" I asked. "Will Mother discover me gone? She'll be so angry." My lip quivered. "She's very unkind when she's angry."

"I can't speak to that. I wish I could, but I don't know. What I can say is this," Professor Gabriel started. "You are unique, Millie Maven. I've never met a child with such potential. When you say the Great Teacher called you, I believe it with my whole heart. I also believe you have much still to see and learn."

He took a step toward me. "I believe you will change this entire place. And I think Soren knows that."

"Soren? What about him?"

"Soren's great skill is his ability to lie. And he will stop at nothing to take you from this place. Consider why else you suddenly have your memories. Believe me, this does not happen."

Millie, tick, tock.

The voice whispered. I glanced to the woods six yards away. Wind rustled the tops of the trees and moved between their leaves. *Soren did lie*, I thought. *He had lied to me plenty already. Could all this be his doing?*

"So it isn't true, what I'm remembering?" I asked.

"Are they just lies from Soren?"

"They may be true memories. I don't know about the life you have outside of FIGS. But I do know the Great Teacher called you here for this moment. I know the enemy wants you to believe you should not be here. Playing on your fears is a very good way to do that."

My panic had settled a bit. Professor Gabriel's logic worked its way into my mind. I was still afraid but no longer blinded by hysteria.

"As always, the choice to stay has to be yours," Professor Gabriel said. "But I encourage you to remember who you are: chosen and called by the Great Teacher, wielding his medallion. Please see this through in spite of your fear, Millie. I promise you will find endless power. Power for the world from which you came."

Softly, as if only for my heart to hear, the Great Teacher's voice rose over the accusing whispers.

I call you chosen, daughter of the red medallion.
This is your path.

His words filled me with warmth and quieted my fears. How quickly fear could rob me of the truth!

"So, Millie Maven, what do you choose?"

I glanced toward the dark woods a final time. I thought I saw a dark figure shuffling between the trees, watching and waiting. That might have been my imagination.

Though I thought it was more.

I turned back to Professor Gabriel and smiled.

"I forgot this was my path. So I think I'll stay."

He smiled brightly. "I knew you would."

I rolled my eyes goofily. "No, you didn't."

"Oh yes, I am very wise and know many things." He gave me a wink and I giggled as we returned together, crossed the invisible wall, and FIGS came back into view.

CHAPTER EIGHT

The next week passed quickly. Each day my worry and fear of my mother diminished. Out of sight, out of mind, so to speak. I had asked Professor Gabriel if my memories would be wiped again. The answer had been no.

At first I was concerned that I would lose my faith again and flee. But as hours then days passed, the opposite happened. My days at FIGS started to feel so wonderful compared with what I knew of the world from which I'd come.

The girls in my dorm prodded me for information about why I'd rushed out of class, but I kept my answers generic. I wasn't ready to divulge everything, except with Mac. She knew every detail.

Doris had tried to get me reprimanded for disrupting class, but Professor Gabriel shut her down quickly.

I understood from the way the other teachers looked at me that they knew what had happened.

We had different classes each day, filled with lessons about how the gifts work. We practiced. I mostly watched, the sneering commentary from Doris constant.

I focused on ignoring her and listened carefully to everything the professors said, hoping something would help me discover my gift. I asked Dean Kyra about it during dinner once and she reminded me to be patient. The Great Teacher had given me the medallion for a reason, and in time I would see why.

I tried to take her words to heart, but it was difficult to see others wield such power while I could only watch.

Mac and Olive, both with Earther gifts, were learning to grow flowers, dozens at a time. Boomer and Collene worked on healing animals in the nearby forest. Adam and Polly, both Quicks, were racing Professor Tomas, who always won. Dash and Gwendolyn, Meats, were throwing boulders back and forth. Doris and Sid, Shifters, were turning water to steam and then to ice. Harvey and Lianna were the only two Benders of the group, and I didn't see them as often as they worked privately with Professor Claudia. On and on. Wonder after wonder. I clutched my red medallion and hoped the Great Teacher would reveal my gift soon.

During dinner on the seventh evening I sat at my usual table with the girls from my dorm. We chatted about the day as we devoured the feast, a rainbow of colorful food set along the wooden serving table. I was getting a second helping of garlic mashed potatoes when my hair lifted off my shoulders and an invisible tug rubbed at the back of my neck.

Instinctively I placed my hand on the spot and noticed it was bare. It shouldn't be bare. The chain that held my medallion should be there. I saw Doris, Dash, and Adam wearing mischievous grins.

My medallion dangled from Adam's hand. He was getting fast. I hadn't even seen him coming. I set down my plate and dropped my eyes to slits.

"Give it back," I demanded.

In my peripheral vision I saw Mac stand. Boomer joined her.

"Why do you even want it?" Doris asked. "It does nothing."

I took a step toward them, heat spreading down my back. "It's mine."

"'It's mine,'" Dash squeaked, mocking me. "Come and get it then, chosen one."

Doris let a cruel chuckle fall from her mouth. She took the medallion from Adam and placed the red circle in her palm.

"Bet I can melt it before you can take it," Doris threatened.

"Stop it, Doris," Mac spat. She'd moved to stand beside me.

"Or what?" Doris asked. "You'll flower me to death?"

Adam and Dash laughed.

I could feel Mac's anger and felt the same.

"I can do more than grow flowers," Mac threatened.

"And she's not alone," Polly said, stepping beside me.

"Yeah," Boomer said, moving in with Harvey.

On cue, Gwendolyn, Ciara, and Sid moved to stand with the Elite twins.

"Perfect," Doris said. "Let's see who's stronger, your friends or mine."

Her confidence was not misplaced. Her group comprised students with powerful physical abilities. Shifters, Meats, Quicks. They were stronger and faster. I loved my friends, but they were mostly Healers and Earthers. And I had nothing to offer. I was afraid of what the Elite group would do to us.

"Bring it on," Mac said, ready to take Doris down. The air was tense as we faced off.

"Mac," I whispered, putting my hand on her arm. The familiar sense that this wasn't the way nipped at my heart. But before I could say anything else something whooshed by me.

Polly, a Quick, raced toward Doris, her aim the medallion. Dash saw her and extended his arm so that Polly's chest collided with his stiff palm. The impact stopped her cold and knocked her off her feet and into the air. She flew back toward us and crashed to the hard floor.

"Polly!" Lianna cried and rushed to her friend's side.

"Too slow," Adam teased.

Lianna stood, the quiet girl's eye ablaze with anger. She focused all her energy on Adam and his smile started to fade. As if an invisible force had filled his chest, his face turned dark. His eyes filled with tears and he started sniffing.

"Leave him alone, you little creep!" Ciara said, stepping up to comfort Adam.

"You started this!" Boomer yelled. He and Harvey were helping Polly to her feet. Her face was scrunched in pain. Others were on the point of breaking. The room would lose itself to chaos.

"And we will end it," Doris sneered. She turned her eyes on my medallion.

"So," a commanding voice rose above the rest. Dean Kyra entered the mess hall, professors in tow. "You have chosen division." Her voice was calm as always. "Miss Elite, please return Miss Maven's medallion to her."

Doris exhaled, frustrated. She held out the medallion but dropped it to the ground before I could clutch it.

"Oops," she said. Mac flinched and I knew she needed all her strength not to slap the evil twin.

Dean Kyra didn't flinch, confirming that when she said we would learn on our own, she meant it. So what was the lesson here? I felt wronged. I scooped up my medallion and secured it around my neck.

"I think it is time," Dean Kyra said. She glanced at the professors and received simple nods of agreement.

"Time for what?" Mac asked.

"The next trial," Dean Kyra answered.

CHAPTER NINE

Dean Kyra and the professors led us from the dining room, across the entryway, and down the wide east hall. They stopped across from the library in front of a padlocked door. I'd noticed it on my first day. Was this where our second trail would begin? Nervous energy pulsed in the air, and fear began to build in my chest.

"The second trial is called the Trial of Shadows," Dean Kyra began. "It will happen in a place known as the Shadowlands." She motioned to the locked door behind her. "Your path to the Shadowlands is through this door."

She dropped her hand and tucked it behind her back. "You have one objective: to get the golden vial that sits in a cave at the top of Shadow Mountain. First you will face the dungeons running underneath the institute. Second, you must cross the marshland between you and the mountain. Finally, you'll scale the mountain's narrow path and find the cave where the golden vial rests. This trial will be done as a group. There is only one golden vial, and unless it is found, you all fail."

A quest challenge, I thought. Mac looped her arm through mine.

"Know this," Dean Kyra continued. "The Shadowlands are designed to test you. They will bring out the fear and darkness within you. Though your objective is to collect the vial, your purpose is to see one another clearly."

She watched us carefully. "Only one who is pure of heart can collect the golden vial. Division and distrust will taint the purity you must protect."

"This does not sound good," Mac whispered to me, glancing at Doris.

My thoughts exactly.

"Fear and darkness will affect your gifts in the Shadowlands," Dean Kyra said. "So you must not rely on them fully. Instead, look to one another for help. Above all, guard your hearts, for there you will discover the true treasure."

She motioned for Professor Alexandria and Professor Tomas to hand out small backpacks gathered against the back wall. I hadn't noticed them before. They were uniformly black, all the same size. I counted twenty-one.

"Inside these packs you will find all you need for primitive survival. Plenty of food and water. You will not die from hunger or thirst." She said it like it was supposed to be funny. It wasn't. Professor Tomas handed a backpack to me, and I slipped it on. Light and comfortable.

Dean Kyra nodded toward the door and Professor Gabriel lifted a key to the padlock.

"To recap: navigate the dungeons, cross the marsh, climb the mountain, find the golden vial. You have three days. If at the end of the three days the golden vial has not been recovered, then you will have failed the Trial of Shadows." Dean Kyra paused. "Fail and you will all leave FIGS to return home immediately."

Shock and disbelief rippled through the students. Leave FIGS? An image of my mother floated through my mind. My fear escalated.

Dean Kyra raised her hand and the students quieted. "Do not worry. I believe in you all." But her words didn't ease my worry, and judging by expressions it didn't ease anyone else's either.

Professor Gabriel opened the iron door. Lanterns along the walls illuminated a narrow staircase plunging into darkness.

"The steps will take you to a round domed atrium and a set of double doors," Dean Kyra started. "The dungeons are through the doors."

"How will we know the way out?" Olive asked.

"All will be discovered," Dean Kyra said. "Just follow the path."

Cryptic, which meant it was going to be harder than she made it sound.

"There is one more thing," she said. "Once you leave the atrium, we will not be able to help you for three days, or until you recover the golden vial. If you find yourself in mortal danger, you will have only each other."

"But you won't let us die," Mac asked. "Right?"

"There will be no help, no matter the consequences," Dean Kyra said.

"You're saying we could die down there?" Boomer squeaked.

"You can't actually let us die, can you?" Polly asked.

"This is crazy!" Ciara said.

"I'm not going to go if I might die!" Collene said.

"And as always, Collene," Dean Kyra said, "that is your choice."

That brought us all to silence.

"If you believe you are not ready, you do not have to go," the dean said. "But you must leave FIGS with no memory of this place. If you want to continue the program, then you must face the Trial of Shadows."

I considered her offer. Would I really rather risk death than return home? Would any of us? Professor Gabriel smiled at me. He didn't look afraid at all, as if he knew something about me that I didn't. I wished I had his confidence.

"The choice is yours," Dean Kyra repeated. "But I urge you to set aside your fear for the promise of freedom you will find if you continue. A power that is greater than your gifts. A power that will change the world."

My mind gave me good reasons for leaving. Death was at the top of the list. But my heart had been touched by the Great Teacher. Though afraid, I reminded myself I had been called here. I had been given the red medallion and had yet to understand why. I couldn't leave till I knew.

I released Mac's arm and walked to the open door. The path was dark and steep, and I swallowed my fear. I felt a hand touch my arm. Mac had joined me, and soon Polly, Boomer, and Harvey too. One by one, every student followed my lead.

We were ready.

"Remember, only those with pure hearts can find the golden vial," Dean Kyra said. "Division will be your enemy. Work together. And be careful. The Shadowlands hold many dangers. May the Great Teacher guide you all."

I looked back at the dean.

She gave a small nod and I started the descent.

CHAPTER TEN

I descended the narrow staircase, leading the charge even through my knees rattled with nerves. I stepped into the atrium, round and domed just as Dean Kyra had said. Torches jutted from iron sconces along the walls, and straight ahead stood a set of double doors. The rest of the students filed in after me.

"What do you think's behind there?" Mac asked at my side.

Given our history with the trials so far, it probably wasn't Candy Land. I shrugged and felt my nerves travel from my legs to my fingers. I started to reach for the door handles when someone knocked my shoulder and pushed through Mac and me.

"Move, Misfit," Doris said, Dash right behind her.

"Ouch," Mac said. "What's the deal, Doris?"

"You two aren't equipped to go through first," Doris snapped.

"She doesn't even have a gift," Dash finished.

I was getting tired of their heckling. But I was afraid to go through. We had no idea what was on the other side. The Elite twins didn't waste any time. In sync they each pulled a door open to reveal a dark pathway. Seeing how dark it was, Dash lifted a torch from the atrium wall.

"I'm going to be the first one to that golden vial, Misfit," Doris hissed over her shoulder.

"This isn't a race," Mac replied. "Dean Kyra said it's a group trial."

"Teachers always say that, but what they're really waiting to see is if someone steps up and leads." She faked a shocked expression and directed it at me. "You didn't think it was going to be you?"

Dash snickered and the two stepped into the dungeon, their flame licking the air.

More kids pushed by Mac and me, bumping my shoulder as they moved. The Elite lackeys, with another torch, followed their leaders without question. Mac stepped back to my side as others dared enter, torches in hand.

"Ignore them," Mac said.

"Ignore who?" Boomer appeared beside me with Harvey and Lianna. I didn't see Polly or Olive. They must have already gone in. We were the last in the atrium.

"Doesn't matter," Mac said. She took several long steps and grabbed one of the last torches. "Let's go." She glanced at us. "Stay together."

We nodded, and Harvey grabbed a second torch as we moved into the dark dungeons. Mac shined the firelight over the space. The tunnel was hewn from stone, curved across the top, an arm span wide and twice as tall. It split; we could go right or left. Huddled together, we chose right.

A couple yards down the path on the left, I noticed a door with a small barred window above my eye level. Mac moved the torch and looked inside. I rose to my tiptoes and placed my head next to hers.

Beyond was a square prison room, which you would expect in a dungeon. What I didn't expect was the wooden desk sitting in the middle with a book laid on top, an ink jar, and a quill beside it. I could barely make out the title.

"*Book of History*," I whispered.

"Weird," Mac whispered.

"Yeah," I replied.

"Come on, guys," Boomer said. "I don't like this place."

Mac and I stepped away from the door and led the group onward. The fire blazing in the torches gave off a wide circle of light. We passed more prison doors every five yards or so as we traveled deeper into the dungeon. I heard Harvey jiggling the handles of each one as we passed. Locked. All of them.

A cold sensation nipped at the back of my neck, raising the hairs there. What kinds of things had happened here? Why did a school for gifted students have a dungeon? Could you end up here if you broke the rules? Was there anyone still in here?

Ahead of us the path split once more.

"Oh man," Boomer complained.

Mac came to a stop at the intersection. "I think we should go right."

"No," Boomer said. "Last time we followed you I almost got eaten by plants. We should go left."

Mac rolled her eyes. "Fine. Lead on, Mr. Talley."

He swallowed, looked down the dark path and turned his eyes back to Mac. "You should go first," he said. "You have a torch."

Mac shook her head and moved, the group on her heels. We traveled another dozen yards, following the flow of the path we had chosen. I was making a mental map in my head in case we needed to get back. I stayed close to Mac with Lianna beside me, while Harvey and Boomer walked a few yards behind.

"I wonder where everyone else is?" Lianna asked. "Don't you think we should be running into people?"

She had a good point.

"Maybe we went the wrong way," Harvey said.

"Like I said," Mac started. "Should have gone right."

"Great!" Boomer snapped. "Blame the chubby—"

A thud and painful groan snuffed his words out. Mac, Lianna, and I whirled around to see Boomer on the floor rolling over onto his side from his stomach. I rushed to him and bent to help him up.

"Are you okay?" I asked.

"Yeah," he groaned. "I tripped."

He placed his hand on my shoulder and I heard it squish against my sleeve. Something cold began to soak the fabric and wet my skin. "Ahh," I said.

"What?" Mac asked.

"There's something all over my hands," Boomer said. "It's goopy."

"Gross," I said.

"Sorry, Millie." Boomer wiped his hands on the stone wall once and then pulled back. "Man! There's more on my hands now."

He turned to us. "It's all over the wall."

An icky shiver shook my body. I didn't want to know what it was. I just wanted to get away from it.

"Boomer, what are you doing?" Mac asked.

The boy was sniffing the tips of his fingers. "It smells . . . I don't really know how to explain it. I wonder what it is."

"Just wipe it on your pants or something," Mac ordered.

Boomer's gaze was completely focused on his palms. He stuck his pointer finger in his mouth and licked it clean.

Lianna gasped and threw her hand over her mouth.

Harvey took a step back.

I stared wide-eyed, and Mac shouted, "Are you kidding me, Boomer?"

He looked at her, his face doused in torchlight, and smiled. "I've never tasted anything like it." He stuck three more fingers into his mouth and yanked them out clean. "Kind of bitter, but then . . ." He started licking his palm.

Mac yanked Boomer's hand away from his mouth. The rest of us were frozen by the scene.

"Boomer, you have no idea what that is!"

His eyes were wide as saucers and they danced in the torch blaze. "I want more."

"No! Boomer, we have to keep moving," she said.

I noticed Harvey stepping toward the wall where the goop hung. He leaned toward it. "It's interesting," the tall boy said.

"Harvey, don't."

He nodded at me and stood, but I saw his eyes flicker to the goop more than once.

"Now, Boomer," Mac said. "We need to get out of here."

"Okay." He yanked his wrist free from Mac's hold. "I'm coming." Mac led us, and I watched Boomer lick his other hand clean as he followed. My stomach turned, but as we got farther down the tunnel, I started to smell something alluring in the air.

The walls shimmered with goop. It piqued my curiosity. What could it be? I couldn't ignore it. I almost wanted to taste it for myself. I could sense Lianna and Mac were curious as well.

Boomer pushed his way forward and took the lead.

"Wait, Boomer," Mac said. The boy turned around, smiling like a fool. His laugh echoed through the stone tunnel. "Don't be afraid," he started. "Boomer knows the way!"

"What?" Mac questioned.

"I can feel it," Boomer said. His eyes were wide and wild. "I can feel everything."

"You aren't acting like yourself," Mac said, worried.

"I'm better!" He yelled. He laughed crazily for a few moments. "I need more goop. I will lead us to it."

He rushed out of the large circle our light provided.

"Boomer!" I called. Mac and I raced after him, Lianna and Harvey behind us. We soon caught him in the torchlight a few paces ahead, and after a moment he slowed.

Mac stopped cold. I nearly bumped into her. Lianna screamed as terror washed over her face. My mind tried to comprehend what I was seeing.

Worms covered the floor, clung to the side walls, and inched across the ceiling, leaving shimmering goop in their paths. The gargantuan worms were ten feet long and several inches thick. I counted more than a dozen.

I struggled to breathe. To think.

"This is where we need to be," Boomer said, reaching for the nearest worm and running his fingers through the tracks of shimmering slime.

"This will set us free," he whispered.

My heart was still racing from what I saw with my own eyes.

Worms. Real, moving, gigantic worms.

And we were stuck in the dungeon with them.

Chapter Eleven

My brain panicked as the giant worms continued along their paths. They hadn't reacted to Lianna's screaming and seemed completely unaware we were there. Or maybe they didn't care. I finally found my breath.

"What the . . ." Mac whispered, her face pale, the torch trembling.

My eyes were trying to convince my brain that what I was seeing was real. Giant worms. Or slugs. Creatures that shouldn't exist. Were they dangerous? The sight of them felt threatening and I didn't want to stick around to find out.

"Boomer!" I called. "We have to get out of here."

"No way," Boomer growled. "I came here for them."

He worried me.

"Boomer, they're monsters." Mac's voice was thin.

"Don't worry. They seem nice. And guess what?" He plopped the finger he'd dragged through the shimmering slime into his mouth and licked it clean. "They make the goop."

Reality slammed against my skull. "You're eating..."

"Worm sludge," Harvey said. He, too, was pulling his fingers from his mouth. He shook his head from the taste, scrunching his nose in disgust. But a second later he was stroking his finger back through the clear goop that stuck to the wall.

He sucked his slime-covered finger dry, paused, then held out his torch for me to take. "I need more fingers," he said.

I hesitantly took the light, unsure what else to do. Mac was shaking, eyes plastered to the fleshy worms. Lianna sniffed beside her. Fear leaped in my chest and threatened to knock me off my feet.

We had to get out of here. We'd get stuck in these tunnels if we didn't. The goop made people act differently, and it made them desperate for more.

I had to do something. I carefully pulled Lianna and Mac away from the boys, who were devouring goop like it was candy. I dropped my voice to hide my words from Boomer and Harvey.

"We have to get out of here or we'll get stuck," I said.

"We need to stick together. Whatever happens, we cannot eat the goop."

"I hate worms!" Mac squeaked. I'd never seen her so afraid. "Do you think there are more in the tunnels?"

I had to be brave. But how was I supposed to be if Mac couldn't? She was braver than most. I pushed my fear aside. "I don't know," I said. "But let's not stay here and find out."

She nodded. "And the boys?"

I turned to them. "Boomer," I called.

"I'm not leaving!" he yelled back, now dropped to a squat near a worm on the floor. "Go on without me."

"You can't stay here. We have to get to the Shadow-lands and get the golden vial," I said.

"That's a lie," he yelled. "I know things now. I know that's a lie."

The goop was messing with his mind. It was danger-ous. I glanced at Mac and saw her staring at the wall beside her. Slime was sliding down it. Lianna was watching too. If I didn't get us out of here, we'd all be goners. I needed a plan.

How was I going to get them all to follow me? What did Boomer want most right now? Goop. So did Harvey. And I just needed Lianna and Mac not to touch the stuff. An idea clicked and although I wasn't sure it was very good, I had to try.

"Mac, Lianna," I whispered. "I need you two to hold hands, okay? Mac, you have the torch. You can't let it go, okay?"

They agreed. Mac interlocked her free hand with Lianna's and I did the same. With Mac and me on either side of Lianna, torches in hand, we'd have to release something to touch the slime. Hopefully this would keep us clean. "Follow my lead," I whispered to them.

"Boomer—"

"Go away, Millie!" Boomer said. Harvey had joined him near the worm on the floor.

"I know where even better goop is," I lied.

"Liar."

"Fine, stay here. But when we have all the good stuff, don't come crying," I said. My voice was forced and my fingers were shaking. This was never going to work. But Boomer slowly turned his head to look at me and Harvey did the same.

"Where?" Boomer asked.

I swallowed. "You have to come with me to get it."

"Just tell me where it is and I'll go myself."

"No, I don't trust you not to take it all."

His eyes flickered to Harvey and then back to me.

"How do I know you're telling the truth?" Boomer asked.

"You don't," I answered. "But stay here and I promise you'll be missing out." I prayed he couldn't hear the thundering of my pulse.

"I get first bite!" he snapped. His eyes were darker than I remembered them.

"Fine," I said. "This way." I swallowed, holding Lianna's hand tightly, and stared down the tunnel with worms. I walked quickly, pulling Lianna and Mac along with me. We couldn't go back. Back would take us to the starting point, and we needed to get *through*. Forward was the only option. As least I hoped.

Five paces down, then ten. I hoped to leave the worms behind, but every dozen feet or so more appeared, clutching the ceiling and inching along the walls. Boomer and Harvey were still following, occasionally swiping goop from the walls with their fingers.

I continued to lead, trying to calm my panic. Why had I taken over? I wasn't suited to lead. I thought I felt a breeze against my cheek and held my breath, hopeful, but nothing came. Wishful thinking?

"What is it? Are we there?" Boomer asked.

Before I could answer I heard giggling from up ahead. Just beyond my torch. The laughter came again, followed by the breeze. It hadn't been wishful thinking. Follow the breeze, find an exit. Simple enough.

"Millie?" Mac whispered. "Did you hear that?"

"Yeah," I answered, and I knew what it meant. Someone else had discovered the goop. I moved carefully down the tunnel. There were more worms and more goop. The giggling became louder, and after a dozen more strides I saw a crouched human with dark hair, the ends dyed pink.

"Polly?" I said. She waved and shoveled a palm full of sludge into her mouth. Beyond her, more students were pushing their fingers and hands deep into the worm sludge. Eight in all, surrounded by goop and long fleshy worms.

I froze. Where were the others who had come into the dungeons with us? Were they stuck somewhere else, feasting on worm slime? Terror pressed against my chest and I forced a breath through it. I could leave them all. What other choice was there? Leave them. No, Dean Kyra had said we were supposed to do this together. Of course I couldn't leave them.

"Come with me and you can have all the sludge you want!" I yelled. That captured the attention of most. "I know where the sweetest slime is. You think this stuff is good, just wait."

"How do you know?" Polly challenged.

"Because . . ." I ran through thoughts like water. I

needed to play on their delusions and desperation. "I have the red medallion. And it leads me to treasure. That's my gift."

"Really?" Polly stood.

"Keep it up, Millie," Mac whispered. "It's working."

"Really. Come with me, and I'll prove it," I said.

They looked at each other. They were considering it.

"But I get first bite!" Boomer yelled, cutting in front of me. "That was the deal."

"There's enough for everyone!" I said too excitedly. They didn't seem to notice.

"Well," Polly said, stepping over a worm as if she wasn't bothered by it in the least. "Let's go, girl with the red medallion."

They all stood as I moved through them. I had felt the breeze and knew we just had to keep going. It was the best shot we had. I moved as quickly as they would follow, glancing back to make sure they were coming.

Around another corner, the tunnel looked brighter than the rest. Outside light? It had to be. I released Lianna's hand.

"Go toward the light," I said to her and Mac. "I'll make sure we don't lose anyone."

"Millie—" Mac started.

"Go!" I insisted.

She nodded, still in hand with Lianna, and ran.

"Come on, this way," I said to the others. "We're almost there."

I kept my torch high as we came to the tunnel's end. It curved to the left and at the end was a hole to the outside. I thought I might burst with relief. I just had to get them out now.

"This way," I shouted.

"Wait!" Polly cried. "That looks like leaving."

"Yeah," Boomer said. "The worms are in the dungeon."

"Yes," I said, "but the good stuff is outside."

They looked at each other.

"Come on!" I urged. "You don't want to get stuck in here with this stuff."

I continued, hoping they would follow. None did. They just stared suspiciously. I had lost them. I was about to beg and plead when Mac rushed back inside, breathless.

"I found it!" she yelled, her voice echoing through the tunnel. "Just like she said. Piles of goop. Man, oh man, you have to come see!" She charged back out into the open. The others looked at one another and then raced toward the exit.

I brought up the rear as we ran out into the light

of day. The sky was bright and I squinted against the light. The group scrambled after Mac as she led them away from the tunnels. I didn't know where she was taking them.

The landscape was unlike anything I had ever seen. Packed red dirt lay between the dungeon's exit and what looked to be a lake. But it wasn't a lake, at least not all of it. I could see patches of land, some round and others long paths that cut the surface of the water. Tall gray-trunked trees with huge roots and thin branches grew from the water.

The trees were few and sparse. Moss grew on the bark and hung from the lowest branches. A light mist sat in the air, and it smelled like mildew and the dungeons. The strange smell worried me, but I didn't linger on it because I was so happy to be out.

This is a marsh, I thought. I had seen one in a geography book Mother made me read. The large damp wetland stretched for miles. Far on the other side, a rocky dark mountain rose to a single pointed tip and pierced the clouds.

All of us slowed to a stop. My eyes went back to Mac. She threw me a wink and I smiled. She must have sensed I was having trouble. She'd come just in time.

"Where is it?" Polly demanded.

"I don't see any goop, Mac," Boomer spat.

"Well," Mac started, "that's because there isn't any."

Outrage pulsed through the group.

"What?" someone yelled.

"You lied! I knew it!" said another.

"Let's go back!" Polly called out.

The group turned toward me, and I watched panic take over their faces.

"No!" someone yelled.

I turned around. The dungeon was gone. Vanished. All that remained was red dirt that went on as far as I could see. Feet thundered past me as the hungry students rushed to where the dungeon should have been.

"This can't be happening!" another cried.

Mac and I exchanged a relieved look. At least we wouldn't have to chase after them back into the tunnels.

"How did you know to come help me?" I asked.

"When you didn't show up for a couple minutes I worried. So I came to check and figured if I backed up your story it might persuade them."

"Thanks."

Wind lifted the ends of my hair from my shoulders. Suddenly another figure was standing beside me. "Adam?" I said.

"The tunnels are gone," he said, staring at my frantic group.

"You got through?" Mac said.

"Yeah, with the twins and the rest," he said. "We came through a bit ago and have been trying to keep Doris from getting back to the sludge."

So she was infected too.

"I'll go tell them it's safe," he said and then rushed away quickly enough to vanish.

"Everyone is through," Mac said. "Maybe that's why it disappeared."

We didn't have long to ponder this because the desperate crowd turned our way.

Boomer cut through. "Why did you do this?" he hissed at Mac.

"Why?" Mac said. "You were eating worm sludge! You were acting like a loon."

"You had no right!" Boomer shouted.

"We saved you," Mac said.

"We didn't need to be saved!" Boomer yelled directly into Mac's face but the girl didn't cower.

"There has to be a way back," Polly said.

"We can't go back," a voice boomed. Dash, who was clutching Doris's forearm with Adam, and the rest of the group appeared from behind a tree. They walked on the high ground through the marsh waters. "We have to get the golden vial."

"That's a lie," Polly said.

Boomer had said the same thing. The goop was toying with their minds.

"That's the slime talking," Dash said. "Don't forget about the second trial." Doris yanked her arm from her brother's hold. She didn't seem as frantic as the others. She threw her bother an angry look but was breathing more evenly than Boomer, and her eyes weren't as wild.

She'd been out longer. Ingested the sludge a while ago. A spark of hope lit my gut. Maybe they all just needed time.

"Drink some water," Dash said. "It seems to help." He offered his sister the canteen from his pack, but she refused it and walked to the closet marsh pool. Others joined her as the group spread out.

Those who'd feasted followed Doris to the edge of the pool as though each one sensed the others were going through the same thing. They whispered among themselves mournfully, believing something precious had been taken from them.

Those who had skipped the afternoon snack wandered over toward Mac and me. Dash and Adam had been spared, plus a handful of others.

"How did you guys get out?" Mac asked.

"I threw Doris over my shoulder and hauled her out," Dash said. "You guys?"

"We lied to them," I said. "Told them we had better slime out here."

Dash shook his head, and for a moment he didn't feel like my enemy. The moment was brief.

"This is your fault, Misfit," Dash said.

"Are you kidding me?" Mac spat.

"We should have stayed together," he barked back. "Then maybe we could have stopped so many of them from getting into the slime."

"You, Doris, and the lackeys took off without us," Mac said.

"Careful what you call me," Adam said.

"Stop it!" I said. "If we keep doing this, we are never going to get to the golden vial."

Mac and Dash said nothing. A moment of tense silence passed.

"It'll be dark soon," Dash said. "We should make camp here."

I glanced at the sky, noticing for the first time that the sun was sinking low.

"We don't have time for that," Adam said.

"Are you saying we should head into the marsh in

the dark with more than half our group in whatever state that is?" Dash said, motioning to the group still mourning their loss. He made a good point.

"It should only take us a day to cross the marsh," Dash said, "even at a normal pace." Adam nodded his agreement. "We camp here tonight."

After giving the order he leaned in just inches from my face. "Stay away from my sister," he said in a low, cruel tone. Then Adam followed him back toward Doris.

"Jerk," Mac whispered.

Dean Kyra's words floated through my mind. *Division will be your enemy.*

I exhaled. We were doomed.

CHAPTER TWELVE

I woke early the next morning. Without warning, I shot up from a nightmare—or dream. I couldn't remember. My breathing was rapid, my heart racing, my skin on edge. The sun barely showed its face in the east, tucked behind dark clouds.

My head was pounding. I rubbed my temples with my fingers in hopes of relieving the pressure. *I must have slept poorly*. Maybe the cold ground underneath my sleeping mat was to blame.

I forced a deep breath, then exhaled. The sky was gray, lined with the promise of rain. All around me, the students were still asleep on their individual mats. Tendrils of smoke rose from the firepits we'd made the night before. Mist hung in the air and left my blanket a bit damp.

Our group had been divided the night before between those who'd ingested sludge and those who hadn't. I had hoped that with time the feasters would return to their old selves, but most had remained on edge. Mac had stopped trying to talk with Boomer.

We had all been exhausted and had only two more days to get the golden vial. Last night, Dash had sent Adam out to find the best path across the marsh. He'd returned with good and bad news. A path of high ground led all the way around the marsh to the base of the mountain, but it was more than ten miles, and we would need to cover the distance in one day.

If we cut straight across the middle, we could carve off nearly two miles, but that meant traveling over water. We believed this was something we could do with the gifts we had. We'd tried to involve the whole group in the planning, but the response from those who'd eaten the slime had been underwhelming. They hadn't been in the mood for it. They had been tired, dazed, even depressed. They had just wanted to be left alone.

Those of us with clear minds had decided we'd ask again in the morning after everyone had rested. I hated the way Boomer had kept looking at me. Like I'd betrayed him.

I stretched my arms and stood from my sleeping mat, hoping he would wake with some clarity of mind and remember I was one of his best friends. The early morning air was chilly, so I walked to the fire in search of warmth. A few embers glowed in the pit, so I dropped to a squat and extended my hands close to them.

I thought I heard something splash in the distance and turned to look. The marsh was eerie, dim in the still morning. I worried about what we'd encounter as we traveled through. The dungeons had been only the first challenge. And things at FIGS usually escalated.

I noticed another empty mat just north of the firepit. I searched the sleeping faces I could make out, doing a head count in my mind. Worry crept into my gut and I stood. I carefully moved through the sleeping forms to confirm my suspicion.

Mac, Polly, Dash, Adam, Lianna . . . I noted who was present. The only face missing? Doris. The chill of morning seeped through my skin. Where could she be? What if something had happened to her? For a moment I just stood there, caught in fear. *I should wake the others.* What if she'd been taken by someone?

Or something.

I swallowed.

The splash of water, this time closer, drew my attention again. A person, a gray silhouette formed by the weak sun, approached camp from the marsh, just beyond three slender trees with wide, sprawling roots.

Long black hair settled on her shoulders.

Doris.

I watched as she stepped over an exposed root and sloshed through water a few inches deep. She was alone, casually walking toward us. Nothing appeared to be wrong. Where had she gone?

I heard others begin to stir as the clouds parted and the light of the sun came through like a natural alarm clock. I thought I should confront Doris, but I didn't want to start the morning with conflict.

Besides, she wasn't my responsibility or problem.

The thought caught me off guard and the pounding in my head returned. I really must not have slept well.

I moved back to my mat, my curiosity firing on all cylinders. Lianna, on the mat left of mine, yanked her wool blanket up over her eyes while Mac, on the mat to my right, sat up, rubbing her tired eyes.

I looked for a distraction to get my brain to back off the suspicious cliff it had climbed. I spotted Boomer with Harvey and some other boys west of the firepit. He must have sensed me watching and turned to meet my gaze.

I offered a smile and small wave. He didn't wave back and turned away. It was like a punch to the gut.

"I hate sleeping on the ground," Lianna mumbled, yanking the blanket back and sitting up.

"Let's just get this stupid golden vial so we can get back to our beds," Mac said.

Mac's harsh words surprised me.

"You okay?" I asked.

She looked at me and I noticed dark circles under her eyes. "I'm just tired."

I understood.

Over the next several minutes the entire camp rose. Dash, who'd taken command of the group, began to order people to get a move on. We had a lot of ground to cover. Mac rolled her eyes but did as he said. She knew he was right.

I stole a glance at Doris, who was back with her brother, and wondered if anyone else had noticed her walking back into camp. Something about her behavior sat uncomfortably in my chest. I ignored my unease as I rolled up my mat.

It didn't take us long to gather our things, eat the morning crackers and jerky from our packs, and suit up for the journey. Within fifteen minutes we were gathered, facing the marsh. Dash strode to the front and turned to address us.

"Adam found a way through on high ground," Dash said. "Follow us or stay here alone."

"Who made you boss?" Polly snarked.

"You did, when you slurped down worm sludge," Dash barked.

"Why don't we just cut through?" Doris asked. "I'll make an ice path."

Doris is right, I thought. Based on what Adam had seen, cutting through would be faster.

"Last night you weren't so eager to help," Adam said.

"Well, I woke up feeling better," Doris said coyly. She walked to the water's edge and closed her eyes. We watched the water, expecting it to shift to an icy surface, but nothing happened. Doris opened her eyes, jaw clenched. "It isn't working."

Adam chuckled, which seemed cruel since she was trying to help us get across faster.

I wasn't surprised, of course. Adam was a total jerk. Again I was surprised by my thoughts. I shook my head to clear it.

"Shut up," Doris hissed. Adam laughed harder and Doris leaped toward the boy, hands raised to shove him. Adam saw her coming and tried to dodge her with his speed, but nothing happened. Doris's palms connected with him and he stumbled backward, face shocked.

"I thought you were fast?" Doris mocked.

Adam's eyes cut to slits. He tried to rush her but again moved at a normal rate. "What the . . ." he whispered. His gift wasn't working either.

Watching the scene unfold, Dash moved to a small boulder along the marsh's edge and tried to haul it up over his head. Others started trying to use their gifts as well, but nothing was happening.

"We don't have our gifts," Polly said.

"Why?" Adam asked.

"This place is messing with us!" Mac yelled.

My friend's face was twisted with anger. It was disconcerting, and Dean Kyra's words returned to me.

The Shadowlands will bring out the fear and darkness within you.

Fear and darkness will affect your gifts.

"Maybe it was the worm sludge?" someone asked.

"But I didn't have any," Adam answered.

"Maybe it's the water!" another shouted.

The others bickered and complained as I got lost in thought. This place itself was changing us. The water, the air, the mist. It had stolen the gifts.

"It's the Shadowlands," I said. Heads turned toward me. "Dean Kyra said this place would bring out our fear and darkness. Maybe it took our gifts too."

"*Our* gifts," Doris said. "You don't have a gift to lose, Misfit." She sneered, then giggled. A few others chuckled as well and I felt my face redden.

"Yeah," Dash said. "Why don't you let those who actually have gifts figure this out."

Everyone's eyes agreed, and I dropped mine to my feet. *Remember who you are, Millie,* I tried to tell myself, but I couldn't ignore the self-doubt.

"We're going to get stuck in this place!" Boomer said.

"It's worse than that," Polly said. "We'll die here."

Fear blossomed in my chest and smothered any worry I had about Doris. Panic began to rumble through the group.

"We are not going to die here!" Dash yelled. "We found a path. If we go now we can still make it to the mountain before dark."

"I don't trust you," Polly said, stepping away from the group.

Dash got right in her face. "Fine. Then stay here."

No, division will destroy us. We have to stay together.

"Anyone who wants to find the golden vial and make it out of the Shadowlands, follow me," Dash said, starting off west. A few followed. A few more just stood there considering their options.

Through my fear I turned to Mac. "We have to keep this group together."

"Why? What have they ever done for us?" Mac said.

Taken aback, I had no answer.

She exhaled and shook her head. "Sorry, I don't know why I said that. I feel out of sorts." She looked at me. "I feel like something bad is happening to me and I'm afraid."

"I'm not going to let anything happen to you, okay?"

She nodded but her normal joyfulness was gone. I turned toward Polly and the rest of the hesitant stragglers.

"Polly, we can't just stay here," I said. "We have to find the golden vial."

"I don't feel like it," Polly said.

"That's this place talking," I reminded her. "Dean Kyra said it would affect us, remember? The only way to leave the Shadowlands is to work together and get the vial."

Polly seemed to think about it, as did the others around her. I noticed Boomer wasn't among them.

"Fine," Polly said. "But I won't put up with anyone's attitude. Understood?"

It was a clear threat. Polly had dark circles like Mac's under her eyes. In fact, everyone had them. Did I? A warning went off in my heart. I didn't have time to meditate on it because the remaining students started after Dash, and I followed.

CHAPTER THIRTEEN

We traveled all morning. The marsh was hot and humid. The air stuck to my skin. The high-ground path was so narrow that we had to weave single-file through the scarce trees and brackish waters.

Everyone was on edge, not just those who'd eaten worm sludge. Students barked and yelled at one another. Words were sharp and unkind.

While they snipped at one another, my fear grew. Not only because we were divided but because I could sense the change in everyone.

Even in myself. Something was off.

About five miles into our trek we came across a circle of high ground wide enough for us to spread out. We stopped for lunch. People settled in small groups, ignoring the others.

I pulled food from my pack. A cheese sandwich and an apple. Not exactly what I'd become accustomed to at FIGS. Anger swept down my back. At least they could have packed us good food. I devoured my sandwich for lack of anything else to eat.

A spark of girly laughter floated across the circle. Boomer sat with Doris and Dash. Doris tossed her long hair over her shoulder and smiled at the chubby boy. Dread filled my gut.

He wouldn't even look at me, but he'd eat lunch with *them*. He would rather be with them. I was losing my friend.

"Disgusting," Mac hissed. She, Lianna, and Polly sat with me against a tree. They were staring at Boomer and the Elite twins.

"What's his problem?" Polly asked. Her mouth curled in anger.

"He's mad we pulled you guys from the dungeon," Mac said.

"You didn't pull us," Polly said. Then she turned to drill us with a hateful stare. "You tricked us into leaving."

"You guys are all crazy," Lianna whispered harshly.

Polly grabbed Lianna's sandwich just as she was about to take a bite and threw it into the water.

"Hey!" Lianna yelled. The small girl's face went dark

and she leaped at the tall girl like a spider monkey. The two fell backward and rolled, Lianna pinning Polly underneath her and holding the girl's wrists to the ground on either side of her head. Polly started screaming.

"I was going to eat that, you psycho!" Lianna screamed in Polly's face.

"You're the psycho!" Polly yelled back.

I scrambled to intervene as everyone else just watched.

"Stop," I yelled at my friends. "This isn't you."

I looked back at Mac, who stared with the others.

"Help me!" I called to her.

Lianna cried out in pain and crumpled with a thud to the ground beside Polly. The tiny girl whimpered softly as she clutched her right arm. Polly stood.

Polly turned to me and wiped blood from her mouth. Without a word she walked back to Mac and finished eating her sandwich. Horrified, I dropped to Lianna's side. I rested my hand on her shoulder.

"Don't touch me!" she yelled, yanking from my touch.

"Lianna—" I tried.

She sprang up and I saw teeth marks on her arm, blood pooling in the cuts. Her eyes, underlined with dark circles, filled with tears. "Get away from me."

She pushed herself up and scurried off.

For a moment I thought I should go after her. But why? I offered her help and she didn't want it. She'd rejected me.

No. This is the work of the Shadowlands. I have to remember who I really am. Who they all really are.

I stood. "This isn't who we are," I said as loud as I could. "The Shadowlands are doing this to us. Please, we have to fight this."

"Shut up, Millie." I turned to see Boomer glaring at me. Doris giggled and he smiled.

His words were a slap to my face, and I felt shaky.

I looked back at Polly and Mac, who ate as if nothing significant had just happened. Were they all rejecting me? A shiver of terror rattled my bones. I dropped my gaze. I just had to remember who they were. Who I was.

But even as I thought about the truth, I could feel my mind changing.

What if *this* was who we really were?

If that was true, we were in terrible trouble.

CHAPTER FOURTEEN

The farther we traveled into the marsh, the worse my fear became. Boomer was up toward the front walking with the Elites. Occasionally they'd glance back at me and then laugh among themselves. They were talking about me.

Everyone was talking about me. I felt eyes on me constantly. They were all turning against me. I should have seen it coming. I was the girl without a gift. A red medallion but no special skills. I was the girl with no friends, because who wants to be friends with a loser?

A small voice in my heart tried to speak against my doubt.

Remember who you are, Millie.

Remember what the Great Teacher says about you.

For just a second at a time, I would remember and find a breath of peace. But as afternoon turned to evening, the voice of my heart grew so faint that I couldn't hear it anymore.

Mac walked ahead of me and hardly paid me any mind. She was angry and depressed. She didn't want to deal with my problems. Even she had abandoned me.

No, I reminded myself. *This isn't Mac. This isn't me. This is the Shadowlands.* I noted the warnings Dean Kyra had given: Division would doom us. The Shadowlands would bring out our fear and darkness. We just had to stay together and get the golden vial. Then everything would go back to normal.

But the more time passed, the less Dean Kyra's warnings made sense. My perspective started to shift. Maybe this *was* who we all really were. Dean Kyra had also said this trial would help us see the truth about one another. Maybe the truth was that Mac had never really liked me.

By the time we exited the marsh, fear had consumed me. I was alone. No one understood me. I'd be abandoned by everyone. Worst of all, I deserved it.

We came upon a strip of red dirt, the same kind that surrounded the marsh. It stretched the length of a football field to the base of Shadow Mountain. The steep rocky face vanished into the clouds that hid the mountain's peak. The ascent was dark and menacing and appeared to have no clear path.

Somewhere at the top was a cave that held the golden vial. Somehow we were supposed to get it before nightfall tomorrow. Dread pulsed in my chest. We might as well give up now and go home.

Yes, Millie. Now.

The whisper drifted over my shoulders and I turned back to the marsh. My eyes scanned the backdrop; my heart rammed my chest. The voice belonged to my mother. Fear galloped like a horse over me.

I saw nothing in the marsh and turned back toward the mountain. I must have imagined the voice. I sure hoped so.

We'd walked all day and my legs ached. With half an hour of light left, Dash ordered people to set up camp. We begrudgingly went through the motions: collected firewood, unrolled mats, refilled water canteens.

At one point I noticed Doris and Boomer whispering at the edge of our camp. The mountain shadowed their faces. I wondered what they were talking about. I wished they would talk to me.

"Why are you just standing there?" a voice barked at me.

It snapped me free, and I turned to see Mac at my right side. Her eyes were heavy with smoky circles. Her skin was paler than I remembered. "Do something or move," she said.

"Sorry," I said.

She rolled her eyes and huffed away. Tears collected in my eyes and I told myself not to cry.

The rest of the night passed slowly. I was exhausted and alone. I sat on my mat while others talked and ate. More jerky paired with nuts and dried fruit. The large fire in the center of camp crackled in the dark, sparks lifting into the air. I watched it until my eyes were so heavy that I couldn't keep them open. And I feel asleep.

Something drifted into my sleep and disturbed the stillness. Giggles? Groggy, I opened my eyes and saw the fire was barely burning in the pit. It was still dark. The sound came again and I rose to my elbow. Laughter, yes.

All the other sleeping mats were empty. Fear exploded in my body and I shot to my feet. I was alone in camp.

Once more the laughter came, soft on the night breeze. I moved toward the sound, west, where the marsh and the red dirt met. There was a small stand of spindly trees there, and the volume rose as I approached.

I heard voices among the giggling, muffled but childlike. I ran, entered the stand, and stopped cold. Every one of my classmates was frantically digging in the dirt.

In clumps of two or three, they drilled their fingers deep into the soil, clawing at it like hyper puppies. Two fires had been lit to illuminate the scene, and Doris marched around like a drill sergeant.

"Keep digging!" she ordered. "Whatever you find is yours."

I didn't understand what I was seeing, but Doris must have sensed me watching because her eyes shot up to me and she gasped in delight.

"Millie," she said, throwing her hands up over her head. None of the students stopped what they were doing. I gasped when I saw Mac and Lianna digging together over a hole with Polly.

Mac removed her fingers from the dirt and held them out with a joyous gleam in her eye. Her fingers glistened in the firelight and she shoved them into her mouth. I stepped toward her.

"Mac!"

Her eyes shot up to me and she smiled. "Finders keepers."

That's when I knew what I was seeing. Because I had seen that look before. In Boomer's eyes. In the tunnels.

They were eating worm sludge.

"I didn't want to wake you," Doris said as she stepped over a hunched boy shoveling a handful of soil into his mouth. Dash.

"But I was so hoping you would come." She giggled. I'd never seen Doris so . . . *happy*.

"You were?" I didn't know whether to believe her.

"Oh, yes. Look what I've discovered." She dropped to a squat beside her brother's hole and pulled out a handful of dirt.

Doris walked to me and extended her palm. Goop mixed with red dirt shimmered in her hand. "Amazing, isn't it?" Her wild eyes lingered on her palm.

"It's worm slime," I said.

"Oh, no, sweetie, it's so much more than that. It's . . ." She paused, squinting and thinking. Then a soft sigh left her mouth. "It's love."

"Love?" I asked.

"Yes, it's what love must taste like," Doris said, closing her eyes and savoring the taste. "You should try it."

I had seen the way it made the others act. It couldn't be what she said it was. But then, she seemed . . . different.

"Don't you see?" Doris started. "This is what we were sent here for."

"We were sent for the golden—" I started.

"No! Bigger than that! This is the answer to everything. It'll give us the strength to climb the mountain and complete our quest. It'll give us pure hearts. Because it's love, Millie. Oh, just taste it and you'll see!" Doris whirled in a circle and I nearly laughed. I liked this version of her.

But I knew it couldn't be what she said.

Could it?

Had it not made Polly attack Lianna? Or maybe that was the Shadowlands, and the worm goop could make us normal again. No one was concerned that I had shown up. Like relentless gophers, they cared only about their digging.

"I'm not sure I want to," I said.

Doris sighed and made a frowny face. "Well, I can't make you." She turned back to the group. "But this is what we're doing. So either join us and complete the trial . . . or don't."

"What if you're wrong and it's dangerous?" I asked. "It's worm slu—"

"It's not!" Doris said with a laugh. "I mean, it is technically, but don't think about that. It's a gift. It's salvation. This is what Dean Kyra meant when she said we'd find treasure. It's a trip, sweetie."

I tried to recall what Dean Kyra had meant, what she had even said. The longer I stood there, the more sense Doris made. Worm slime had changed her heart.

She was kind and joyful. Everyone else had been bicker-ing, and now they were working together. Maybe the sludge was something beautiful after all.

"Stand with us, Millie," Doris said. "To stand with us is to stand with FIGS. Stand against us and you're on your own."

I didn't want to be on my own. I didn't want to be alone. I was terrified of loneliness. I wanted my friends back. I wanted to stand with FIGS. I wanted to finish the Trial of Shadows and make Dean Kyra proud.

"Just one bite," Doris said, walking back toward me. "And then let your heart decide, okay?"

Just one bite.

"Come on, Millie," a friendly voice said. Mac had stood up. "Join us."

"Yeah," came another from the left. Boomer. "Join us, Millie."

"Millie, Millie, Millie," Mac started chanting, pumping her fist into the air. Others echoed her call. My name rose into the night sky.

"Millie, Millie, Millie."

Their invitation was a welcome warmth after the chill of the day. I glanced down at the sludge in Doris's hand. It seemed to sparkle and I wanted to try it. I wanted to know what they all knew. I wanted to feel the love that Doris spoke of.

I wiped three fingers through the goop as my name bounced around my ears.

As I raised the slime to my lips, I felt my heart thumping. Excitement ran through me. Yes, this must be what we were meant to find. Without another thought, I licked my fingers clean.

CHAPTER FIFTEEN

The worm slime was bitter at first, a strange flavor I'd never encountered before. It made my nose scrunch, and I nearly spat out the goop. But then it melted onto my tongue and filled the sides of my mouth. It trickled down my throat and into my chest, warm and sweet.

"Take another," Doris said, the others watching quietly.

I wanted another even though it had been bitter. Something about it urged me to try again. I licked a second swipe clean.

The second taste was better. The third made my brain explode with desire. It was the best thing I'd ever tasted. I closed my eyes, smiled, and said, "I want more."

Doris laughed as the group behind me started to applaud.

"Dig away, my dear," Doris said. "Dig away!"

I laughed with her and felt my mind go fuzzy. My brain was light and my body was floating. Not actually floating, but if I had jumped, I might have sailed up into the sky. My skin tingled but my heart was calm.

I dropped to my knees and started scraping the dirt. Everyone else had gone back to doing the same. Searching for beautiful worm goop. I giggled to myself as I dug my fingernails into the ground.

Why had I been so hesitant? I felt full of life. Like I could run up the mountainside and collect the golden vial myself. For several long minutes I dug without ceasing.

Then things started to shift. The warmth cooled off and the sweet taste started to fade. I dug with more desperation, needing another taste. Why was the goodness fading so quickly? I looked up for some solace, but everyone was consumed with their own search.

I just needed to get more; that was all. But I could feel my fear roaring back to life. What if I couldn't find any? What if they kicked me out because I wasn't tripping on love like they were?

My heart raced, and I thought I felt something mushy. I scooped it with my pointer finger and shoved it into my mouth. The welcomed warmth returned, sweet nectar running down my throat to silence my fear.

This time it faded even more quickly. Again I felt desperate to replenish my fix. Why was this happening to me? Everyone else seemed focused and fine, while Doris skipped around telling them to keep up the good work. I felt alone in my suffering.

My heart burned as my panic grew twice as large as it had been. Something was wrong with me. I never should have eaten the sludge. I felt terror, not love.

I grasped my chest as the panic started to spread into my legs. I struggled to breathe. My fear was attacking me.

Now, Millie. Get your wretched self back here now before it's too late.

I gasped. Mother?

I looked around, searching for her. There! She stood in the marsh, yards away. Memories I'd abandoned rushed through me. I heard myself whimper in fear.

Doris looked up but only smiled.

No one else took notice. They were too busy digging. I jumped up, my legs like Jell-O. I wobbled and started inching backward as I stared at the thing I feared most: Mother.

I was lost to the overwhelming fear that said only one thing: *Come home, Millie.*

I had to return. How many days had it been? Way more than five. Did my mother know I was gone? What would she do to me if I didn't go back? I fell off the ledge of my fear and raced away from the dig site.

"Millie, where are you going?" Doris shouted, but she didn't follow. No one did. Terror charged my movements as I blazed back toward camp. In front of the firepit I heard my mother call.

Now, before it's too late!

There she was, just south of camp, watching from the marsh. I couldn't bear it. I was in terrible trouble! I had to hurry!

So I ran. I fled east this time, farther from the group digging for worm slime, along the bank without a clue as to where I was headed. I glanced into the marsh and saw her again, watching me.

Hurry, Millie.

She was everywhere, reminding me of the deep trouble I was in.

Before it's too late!

I pumped my legs like pistons as my crazed terror drove me.

Shadow Mountain rose on my left. The marsh was on my right. Ahead of me was nothing but red dirt. The bright stars and moon guided me . . . straight to her. Out of nowhere she was there, ten yards ahead of me in the middle of the path.

I halted and thought my heart might burst from panic. I turned around and she was there as well. I had nowhere to go. The corner of my eye spotted a cave, small and dark, in the base of Shadow Mountain. Mother wasn't there.

I didn't second guess; I just ran. It was all I knew. I raced for the opening and charged into the cave. I pulled to a stop and nearly collapsed. Struggling to breathe, I placed a hand on the cave wall to balance myself. My head pounded. My pulse raced.

Mother would come, so I pushed on, deeper into the cave, my wild inner voice screaming for me to get home. *Find a way.* Ten paces into the darkness, I spotted light around a corner. I followed the glow, turned, and entered a domed room of stone with a brilliant-blue pool shining in the center.

A portal pool. I knew immediately.

Hurry, Millie. You still have time to save yourself.

I didn't turn around. I could feel her there. Somehow, I knew she had wanted me to find this place. So I could go back. I had to go back. There was no other choice. The longer I delayed, the worse my mother's vengeance would be.

I saw light dancing beneath the surface of the water. I wasn't afraid of it as I had been before. This time I knew I wouldn't drown. I would only be transported back to real life.

Now, Millie. Now!

Tears streamed down my face. Mother would never forgive me for what I'd done. I stepped into the water and waded until it reached my waist. I felt the power pull at me, and I dropped down to my neck.

Good girl.

As the water started to take me, I dared to look back at the woman I feared. But it wasn't Mother anymore. It was Soren. Tall. Muscular. Stronger than me in body and mind. With green eyes at once bright and dark. And I knew in that moment that it always had been Soren, playing tricks with my mind.

He smiled and waved as the water swallowed me. I couldn't scream or move. It was too late. Light surrounded me and everything went black.

CHAPTER SIXTEEN

I opened my eyes. The room around me came in all at once but it took my brain a moment to catch up. Every inch was familiar and terror dropped into my gut. I was in my bed, in my room, in the attic, in Paradise, Colorado.

Sweat clung to my brow and blood pounded in my ears. *Soren* was the first thought that popped into my head. He'd been in the Shadowlands. He'd led me to the pool, disguised as Mother. He'd tricked me.

I saw the time blinking on the digital clock: 1:00 p.m. I jumped up from my bed, panicked. What day was it? Aggie had said five days in the other world would get me home before sunrise, but I'd been at FIGS for almost two weeks. Mother had to know I'd been gone.

Why wasn't I by the pool? How had I ended up back

in my room? Maybe that was the way it worked when you came back.

The reality of it all crashed into me and I nearly fell to the floor. I was back. I had left all my friends. Professor Gabriel, Dean Kyra, the school, the Trial of Shadows. Rebecca and the Great Teacher.

The red medallion. I touched my throat. It wasn't there! I'd given that up too.

Soren had tricked me and now I had to face my mother's wrath. I'd never broken so many rules and to such high degrees. I couldn't imagine what Mother would do to me.

Was any of that even real? What if I'd just awakened from a long dream? I mean, this was real right here in the attic, right? The rest had to have been a dream.

I shook in my boots and noticed for the first time that I was wet. And that I was dressed in clothing from FIGS. So . . . so it had been real? Of course it had. And that meant I was in terrible trouble.

I couldn't go downstairs in these wet clothes. They would only add to Mother's disapproval. I yanked open the suitcase that served as my dresser and found it empty. I'd worn all my clothes to keep warm the night I'd followed Aggie to the cave. I didn't have anything else. Also, I was in my FIGS uniform.

Two things happened at once. First, I knew that

FIGS was real. It had to be. Second, panic seized my chest. How would I explain any of this to my mother? I rushed over to the loose boards on the wall and yanked one free. Then the other.

I carefully glanced out. There was still snow on the ground, and my tracks clearly marched across the yard toward the west fence. Not much time could have passed since I left with Aggie. A couple days of sun or more snow would have covered my tracks.

I pulled my head back inside and replaced the boards as my mind worked out what to do. I could hide up here till dark and try to sneak off again. Could I make it to the cave on my own? Even if I could, I knew I shouldn't.

The longer I was gone, the more trouble I'd be in. If I confessed now, maybe the sentencing would be lighter. The only thing I could do was beg for forgiveness and hope Mother gave it.

The door in the attic floor creaked as it started to lift. I froze. A moment later Martha's head popped up and our eyes met. She stared at me with pity and relief.

"I thought I heard footsteps up here," she said. "Where have you been?"

I didn't know how to answer, but I knew Martha well enough. She would hand me over to Mother immediately. She was too scared of Mother to do anything else.

"How long have I been gone?" I whispered.

Martha huffed. "You foolish girl, how could you not know that?"

"Please, what day is it?"

She closed her mouth in a straight line. "It's December 13."

The day after my birthday. I hadn't even been gone a full twenty-four hours.

"You're in a mess," Martha whispered, and I could see the fear on her face. "Come with me," she said. I didn't want to go, but what other choice was there?

I had nowhere to run. No cards to play or moves to make. Time to pay for my actions. I trembled as I climbed down the ladder after Martha to the mansion's top floor. Though terrified, I followed Martha down to the first floor and into the large dining room. Just last night—or two weeks ago—my mother had destroyed by birthday present here.

I saw her pacing by the bay window, dressed in all white, her gray roots coming through her dyed-blond hair. Looking frazzled, she marched with heavy footsteps in her tiny heels.

She noticed us approach and looked up. Her eyes fell on me and she stopped pacing. She exhaled loudly and strode across the room. My body tensed as she neared but then she wrapped me in a hug. I thought she looked relieved.

I was shocked, and for a brief moment it felt as though she had missed me. Then she pushed me away, disgust on her face, eyes dark and confused.

"What are you doing in those wretched clothes? And why are you wet?"

I had forgotten about my attire.

"Why is she wet?" Mother shouted at Martha.

"I don't know, Mrs. Pruitt," Martha answered.

"Where was she?"

"Her room."

"How did she manage to sneak back into her room? I thought every inch of this house was being monitored."

"I don't know, Mrs.—"

Mother turned back to me before Martha could finish. "Where have you been?" she demanded.

"I . . . I . . ." I couldn't think of what to say. She would never believe the truth.

Fear and anger flashed through her eyes. "Who gave you these clothes?"

"Mother, I . . ." Again, I couldn't form words.

Mother didn't appreciate my silence, and her hand came down hard across my cheek. The sound echoed through the room and pain exploded through my face.

Tears sprang to my eyes and heat gathered where her palm had hit me. Mother had never struck me.

"How dare you break my rules!" Mother growled. "How dare you leave the property!"

"I'm sorry," I mumbled.

"Where did you go?" Mother yelled. "Who did you speak with?"

"I didn't . . . I don't . . ."

Mother grasped my arms, squeezing them close to my sides and digging her nails into my skin. "Answer me!"

I opened my mouth but only silence came out. She shook me hard and tears rolled down my cheeks. Her hot breath and loud words blew over my face.

"You ungrateful, worthless girl! I have given you everything, and you dare to disobey me! Tell me where you were! Now!"

"I was with Aggie!" I cried.

Mother stopped shaking me but didn't release her claws from my arms. Pain pulsed under my skin. "Aggie!" she spat. "What did she say to you?"

"Nothing. Nothing," I whimpered.

"Lies! Tell me what she said!"

"I promise she said nothing, Mother."

She held me for another long moment and then pushed me away. I wavered, then sank to the floor.

Mother was working through something in her mind. I could see it in her eyes and I tried to stop my soft cries.

"Shut up!" she yelled at me. "You deserve no pity."

I bit the inside of my lip and begged myself to stop.

"Lock her in the basement," Mother said to Martha.

"I'm sorry, Mother—" I whispered through tears.

She pointed a judgmental finger at me. "Don't call me that! You don't deserve to call me Mother, not after your sins. Contemplate that while you rot in the basement."

She dropped her finger and swallowed her rage. More composed, she locked her terrifying gaze on mine. "You will never leave this house again. It will be your prison for as long as you are wretched."

Martha stood by silently, eyes on her feet.

"No food until I decide I'm not angry anymore," Mother instructed her. "That will be awhile."

"Mrs. Pruitt, are you sure—" Martha started.

"Are you questioning me?" Mother snapped.

"No, ma'am," Martha corrected.

"Good. Let's not forget about dear sick Abby," my mother said.

Martha's daughter. There was more to their story than I knew.

"Take her," Mother ordered. "I can't stand the

sight of her."

Martha collected me off the floor as Mother left the room, her heels clicking on the wooden floor.

✦

The basement was colder than the attic, with stone walls and a concrete floor. The ceiling was low, making the whole place feel claustrophobic. Dark and scary. I hated being down there. It housed rats and cockroaches of all sizes. The dim overhead lighting flickered but never completely went out. And it always smelled like mothballs.

Mother stored unwanted furniture, Christmas décor, random boxes of stuff, and more down there. In the far corner was a single room built by Mr. Pruitt's father, who'd enjoyed woodworking.

It had long since been cleared out of everything but a heavy worktable and a couple of empty buckets. The door locked from the outside. I'd never inquired why.

Mother had threatened to lock me in the basement before, but I'd always changed my behavior enough to receive a lighter punishment. Martha walked me across the hard floor toward the back room. Her touch was firm but tender as she led me inside.

I sniffed and turned as she let go and stepped out of the room. Our eyes connected for a moment and her mouth opened as if to speak. But then she shut it and closed the door. The heavy dead bolt slid shut and I listened to her work boots shuffle across the floor and thunk up the stairs.

The door at the top of the stairs clicked shut and I was alone. It was a prison, just as Mother had said. An eight-by-ten-foot space, my new eternal home.

I stood there for a while, searching for a way out. But I saw nothing to give me hope. Maybe that's why an outer lock had been installed—so Mother could secure me when my true nature presented.

I climbed up onto the long wooden worktable and pulled my knees up into my chest. Images of FIGS filled my mind. The first time I'd gone through the pool I'd lost my memories of Paradise. It hadn't worked the same way coming back. Fresh tears gathered, and I wished I had lost my memories of FIGS.

Instead I would always be haunted by what I had given up. Because of Soren. Because I'd given in and eaten the worm sludge. Or maybe because I was just not meant to be there.

Dean Kyra had said the Shadowlands would bring out the fear and darkness within us. It did exactly that and defeated me. The red medallion gave me false hope. It made me feel special, but I was just a friend- less orphan girl nobody really loved. My body shivered from the cold and shook with my sobs.

Aggie had been wrong about me.

Dean Kyra had been wrong about me.

I wasn't the girl with the red medallion.

I was just a scared girl with nothing.

CHAPTER SEVENTEEN

There was no way to tell time in the basement. I fell asleep but had no idea how long I'd slept. At some point Martha came with a large mason jar of water but, on Mother's orders, no food. She barely looked at me when she opened the door and set the water on the floor.

I was racked with misery. "Please help me," I whispered.

The old woman didn't even look at me when she answered.

"You know I can't."

It was true. She'd be punished if she went behind my mother's back, but I couldn't stop myself from hoping someone would stand up to her and set me free. Hours passed while I laid on the hard table staring at the ceiling grate.

It was large enough for me to crawl through but just out of reach and screwed shut on either end. I imagined that if Mac were here she'd know what to do. I replayed moments from FIGS over and over.

I cried more, which seemed impossible.

I got angry and wanted to scream.

I hated Doris for tricking me, for being nice to me and convincing me to eat the sludge that made me insane with fear so that Soren could get me to the pool. I was convinced they were in on it together. I hated Soren for using my fear against me. I hated myself for falling for it all.

As more time passed I began to realize I was going to die in that prison. Mother would never forgive me and she would never let me go. And even if she let me out of this room, she would never set me free. I think I started to hate her too.

Martha came again to change out the water. I hadn't touched what she'd left before. "Millie, you should drink something," she said softly.

I didn't respond. I didn't have it in me and I didn't like her very much either. She left and I returned to my self-loathing. More time passed. Things that ached became numb and eventually I ran out of tears. Again I drifted to sleep on the hard wood table.

A soft wind brushed over my shoulders. It was warm and kind and I knew, before opening my eyes, I must have imagined it. My eyes fluttered open, expecting to see the dreary walls of my prison. I nearly jumped out of my skin when I found myself lying in a golden field.

I shot up and frantically looked around. *A dream*, I thought. Tall stalks of wheat reached up to a perfectly blue sky dotted with fluffy clouds. The stalks swayed with the playful breeze and danced under the sun.

I turned over to my knees and pushed up to stand. The field stretched as far as I could see. Beautiful, warm, peaceful. Unreal.

My mind had created something to help me cope with my dark predicament.

A sweet tweet floated through the air. I spun to see a beautiful little blue bird. It began to glide down toward me and I couldn't stop myself from smiling.

"Paxaro," I said and extended my arm for him to land.

He plopped down, his tiny talons poking my forearm, and cocked his head at me. Then he tweeted in sharp bursts as if asking me questions. But I didn't speak bird, so I only giggled at his antics.

"Sorry, dear," a motherly voice said behind me. "He forgets not everyone understands him."

I turned and felt my heart fill. "Rebecca."

The beautiful woman with warm brown hair and warmer brown eyes stood before me. She wore her wide-brimmed sunhat but not her green gardening gloves. Her simple long white summer dress fluttered in the wind and made her look like an angel.

"Hello, Millie," she said in a soothing voice. "I've missed you."

"I've missed you too," I said. Then I remembered this was all a dream and my joy flattened.

"You're not really here," I said.

"Really? Huh. It feels like I'm here," Rebecca said.

"But I'm not at FIGS. So you can't be real."

"You traveled back and forth. Who says I can't do the same?"

My eyes widened. "Can you?"

She smiled and shrugged. "Technicalities aren't important. Would you like to come sit with me?"

I nodded and walked to Rebecca. We sat, tall wheat swaying around us.

"So," Rebecca started, "tell me how the Trial of Shadows is going?"

"It's over," I said, "and I failed terribly."

"Did you?"

"Yeah. I don't really wanna talk about it."

"We don't have to," she said.

But I couldn't stop myself. Something about her presence was so welcoming. Before I knew it I was sparing no detail from the moment we entered the FIGS atrium to the second I turned around and realized Soren had been masquerading as my mother.

"I couldn't keep anyone together," I said. "I tried, but everyone was falling apart in the marsh. Then Doris convinced me to eat the worm sludge. She made me believe it would be okay, but it only made me see how frightened I really am. How alone I am."

I pulled my knees close to my chin and dropped my forehead against them.

"The Shadowlands are no cake walk," Rebecca said. "But it sounds like they did exactly what they're supposed to do."

"Bring out our fear and darkness," I whispered.

"Precisely."

"Why? So we could end up more divided and more afraid?"

"Quite the opposite, actually. So you'd find unity and see each other as one. All of you are the same, you know, afraid of shadows."

"I don't even understand what any of that means." My emotions bubbled up again. I sensed Rebecca watching me.

"You're upset," she said.

"Yes!" I stood and turned to face her. "I'm afraid, and angry, and alone." Tears slipped down my cheeks. "And I don't know what to do."

"All there is to do is remember who you are," Rebecca said. She was calm, unfazed by my outburst.

"I don't know anymore. I thought I did. But you must have made a mistake."

"It wasn't me who chose you, Millie," Rebecca said. "It was the Great Teacher."

"Well then *he* made a mistake. He was wrong about me." More tears blurred my vision. "I'm just so afraid. And I'm not strong. I don't even have a gift. My friends turned on me, and Doris hates me."

"Yes, Doris is troubled."

"She's terrible!"

Rebecca's eye saddened. "Oh, Millie, she *is* you."

"No, we are nothing alike."

"She is reacting out of the same fear you are. She's desperate for people to see her as worthy, but she constantly questions her own self-worth. She's searching for love."

I sniffed. "Really? How do you know that?"

"I know everyone's story," Rebecca said. "And I don't usually share, but Doris is going to need you to see her. To help her. So I will share this: Doris's mother, the one from the world outside of FIGS, is cruel to Doris and

Doris alone."

I knew a thing or two about cruel mothers.

"She expects a lot from Doris, and she favors Dash over her daughter. She puts so much pressure on Doris to be perfect, and when Doris fails, her mother speaks so much hate over her." Rebecca's eyes started to tear up. "Doris feels so inadequate. She copes by hating anything she views as better than her. She's just trying to protect herself. She doesn't realize she's blocking out the only thing that can save her."

"And what's that?" I asked.

Rebecca smiled, her face aglow. "Love, Millie. The love of the Great Teacher. The same love that will save you."

I was speechless for a moment. Doris and I were the same? It seemed impossible, but as Rebecca talked, I saw myself in Doris's story. But my defensiveness came back. "That doesn't make it right, though—the way she's treating me."

"You are not called to judge her, Millie," Rebecca said. "You are called to love her. The Great Teacher says you must love your enemy as yourself. Because she's you, Millie."

"I don't know if I can love her," I said. "I don't even know if I can love me."

"And so we start back with lesson one," Rebecca said.

"Remembering who the Great Teacher says you are."

As it had happened when I was with Rebecca in the FIGS garden, the air filled with an unexplainable presence, and the most comforting voice whispered across the breeze.

Remember the ways I love you.

Remember that I chose you and call you mine.

The golden field seemed to respond to the Great Teacher's voice, dancing and swaying with the winds. With his simple words, all the love I'd forgotten in the Shadowlands came rushing back.

I remembered the way I'd felt sitting under the grand willow in the garden. The way I'd found my confidence during the maze in the Initiation Trial. The Great Teacher gave me the red medallion and called me his own.

How could I have forgotten such deep love?

"We all forget," Rebecca said, still sitting among the wheat. "That's Soren's greatest trick. He's the father of lies, so he'll always try to make you believe you are less than what the Great Teacher says you are. Remembering your true nature is a journey. One you are on."

Rebecca smiled. "And so is Doris."

The voice of the Great Teacher came again, soft and strong.

I am in all. I love all as I love you, Millie, and my love never ceases.

All are created in my image.

As you do unto others, you do unto me, sweet daughter.

I could feel his love for Doris, Dash, Adam, Mac, Boomer, and everyone else at FIGS. The love pulsed through me. It overwhelmed me and brought me to my knees. Hot tears blurred my vision as the intense love washed over me.

"What you are feeling is a fraction of what the Great Teacher feels for you and everyone you encounter," Rebecca said.

The feeling started to lessen. Rebecca had stood and was walking to me. She knelt in front of me and tucked her hand underneath my chin. Her warm eyes blazed with power.

"Don't you see, Millie Maven? You are loved and cherished by the greatest force that has ever been. That created all. He calls you his. You are chosen. And he loves all with the same intensity. Because you are all his. One creation, one people."

She sweetly brushed my hair back behind my ear. Her words began to meld with my heart. "The Great Teacher says to bless those who curse you. Offer them love, for they are the same as you, created in the fullness of the Great Teacher's love. To hate them is to hate yourself. Hate only creates more hate."

She laughed softly, closing her eyes and soaking in the sun. "But love! Oh, sweet girl, love creates more love, and nothing can stand against the love of the Great Teacher." She opened her eyes and smiled. "Nothing!"

I sniffed. My heart still raced in my chest. "But I become so afraid," I said.

"I know, and it will happen again. But when it does, remember the voice of truth that tells you who you are and reminds you of the Great Teacher's love. Because I promise you, when you walk in love, nothing can stand against you. For you walk with the Great Teacher, who cannot be threatened."

The wind swept through again, warm across my shoulders and through the ends of my hair.

Let me tell you the ways I love you, Millie.

I love you more than the light of a million stars.

I call you perfect, whole, washed clean in my death and life. Don't be afraid. I am with you always.

His voice emboldened me and filled me with joy as I began to remember who I was.

Whatever you do to others, you do to me.

Bless those who come against you, because they've only forgotten that they're perfectly loved. Show them,

Millie. Show them my love.

"I will," I whispered.

The wind swirled, wrapping me in love and peace.

"Do you see now?" Rebecca asked.

"Yes," I said. "I see now."

She chuckled and pulled me into a hug that made me cry with joy. She jumped up and yanked me to standing. Paxaro swooped down from the sky and flew between us as Rebecca twirled me around in a funny dance.

The Great Teacher's presence lingered as we giggled and moved. I wanted to stay in that place forever, but I knew I had been called to do more. Eventually we fell to the ground exhausted, yet somehow still invigorated, and laid on our backs, staring up at the white puffy clouds.

Paxaro perched on my stomach. He cheeped loudly when I giggled, then he flew off. For a few minutes we were silent.

"Will I forget the Great Teacher's truth again?" I asked softly.

"Maybe," Rebecca answered. "Life is a series of forgetting and remembering."

I thought maybe I was beginning to understand what that meant.

"But when you do, just search for the voice of truth.

It will always lead you back home," Rebecca said.

I turned my neck to glance at the beautiful gardener. "Who are you really?"

She looked at me. "I'm really a gardener and friend."

She was more than that, I was certain, but I didn't push.

A few more minutes passed and through my joy I remembered my situation. "How am I supposed to get back to FIGS? I'm stuck in Paradise."

"Remember, most people you encounter have forgotten who they really are. Show them love and your heart will be pure. Also, the pool where Aggie led you will send you back."

I sat up. "You know Aggie?"

Rebecca smiled and winked at me. "It's time for you to go."

"I want to stay here with you."

Rebecca sat up as well and placed her hand on my cheek. "Don't be afraid. I'm watching over you, and he's always with you."

I smiled and gave a little nod. The warm sun, the soft wheat, the song Paxaro was singing all made me feel suddenly sleepy. I laid back down while Rebecca softly stroked my cheek. "Sleep well, sweet girl," was the last thing I heard.

I opened my eyes with a start and knew immediately I was back in the basement prison at the Paradise mansion. My heart pumped fear. I closed my eyes and remembered the words of the Great Teacher: *Don't be afraid. I am always with you.*

Even here? In Paradise? I wondered. But somehow I knew he was. I could feel an undeniable love in my chest and knew nothing could separate me from him. I wasn't sure how I knew, but I was certain of it.

I also knew I had to get back to FIGS. I wasn't sure if FIGS was real or just a dream anymore because everything was a bit jumbled, but I was sure that if I didn't return, things here would go very badly for me.

First things first. I had to get out of that prison.

CHAPTER EIGHTEEN

Martha came about an hour after I woke from my dream of Rebecca and the field. I jumped off the table to greet her. The door creaked when she opened it, and she seemed a bit stunned to see me so alert.

"Hello," I said.

"Everything alight?" she asked suspiciously.

"Oh, yeah. I'm great." I realized by the look on her face that she thought I had lost my mind. It was a reasonable thought in the circumstances. But it was hard to contain my excitement after being with the Great Teacher and Rebecca.

"Okay," she said slowly as she walked into the room to replenish my water.

My stomach growled. Martha glanced at me, concerned. "Your mother still hasn't given me permission to bring you food. I'm sorry."

"Don't be sorry," I said. "I know you're just afraid."

She seemed stunned by my words. I too was surprised the words had stumbled out. Rebecca said most people have forgotten who they really are. And I knew Martha was one of those. Her fear had blinded her to love, just as mine had many times. I felt compassion for the older woman in a new way.

When was the last time she had felt love as strong as the Great Teacher's? Had she ever? Could I show her? Even here? Wasn't that what the Great Teacher had called me to do?

"I wish I could help somehow but . . ." Martha continued.

"It's okay," I said. "I know how powerful fear can feel."

Martha swallowed and I thought I saw her eyes glisten with emotion in the dim lighting. "It's just, Abby is sick."

"Is she going to be okay?"

"Not without the medicine the Pruitts pay for."

Now I understood why Martha's loyalty to my mother was so strong. Martha was just doing what she had to for her daughter. I couldn't be upset with her for that. In fact, I realized she was in a type of prison too. In that way we were the same.

She was me as much as Doris was. We were all one

people, made in one image. I felt my heart fill with love for Martha, and I suddenly couldn't contain myself. I went to her and wrapped my arms around her waist, hugging her tightly.

She gasped and stiffened. But a second later she relaxed and laid a single hand on my back. I could hear her heart pounding as I held her for a long moment.

"I'm sorry, Martha. I'm so sorry," I whispered.

The woman sniffed as she patted my back. When I released her I saw a few tears running down her aged cheeks. She stepped back and quickly wiped her face dry. She cleared her throat, embarrassed, and gave a tight smile.

I could tell she wasn't sure what to say, but it was okay.

"I'll talk to your aunt about getting you some food," Martha said. "It's been a couple days. Seems long enough."

"A couple days?" I felt a prick of panic. How would time work at FIGS? What if the Trial of Shadows had already ended? Was I too late?

Then I remembered that the Great Teacher was always with me. I calmed. I couldn't let my fear blind me to what I must do.

"I'll talk to her," Martha said.

"Thank you," I said.

She stared at me a moment longer, a curious look in her eye. "You seem different," she said.

I smiled. "I am different."

Martha gave a tight nod, shook her head, and left, locking the door behind her.

✦

More hours passed. I went through the cycle of forgetting and remembering at least a dozen times: first afraid I'd never get out, then peaceful because I knew the love of the Great Teacher. Even if I didn't make it out, maybe it would be okay.

When the deadbolt shifted and the door squeaked open, I wasn't sure what to expect. I was pleased to see Martha's face again as she pushed open the door carrying a small metal tray.

I could smell the bread and cheese, and I realized how famished I was.

"You spoke to Mother for me," I said.

"I said I would. I do what I say," Martha said. Her voice was warmer than I remembered. I smiled and she returned it. She placed the tray on the floor and cleared her throat intentionally. I looked at her and watched as she glanced up at the large grate in the ceiling. It was a strange thing to do, and I nearly asked her about it.

But she spoke. "Enjoy your food. I made sure to give you everything you should need. Sorry it's so late." Again, peculiar.

I looked at the simple tray, a curious sense filling my bones.

Martha walked out of the room, but before closing the door she turned to me and said softly, "Thank you, Millie."

"For what?" I asked.

Martha shrugged with a sheepish grin. "For being kind."

She shut the door and locked it. The moment she was gone I walked to the tray, picked it up, and carried it to the table. On it lay a single piece of toasted bread, several slices of yellow cheese, and a folded cloth napkin. I unfolded the napkin. A small butter knife had been tucked inside. But I had nothing to spread, so why a knife?

Truth hit me like a train. Martha was giving me a way out!

If I could reach the grate maybe I could use the knife's pointed end to release the screws and crawl out. I shoved a piece of cheese into my mouth and climbed onto the table. I stretched my hand toward the grate but fell short about a foot.

I saw the empty white plastic buckets in the corner of the room. I jumped off the table and rushed to grab one. They were covered in cobwebs and a spider skittered off toward the corner. I hated spiders. Despite my fear, I picked up a bucket and carried it back to the workbench.

I flipped it upside down on the tabletop. It was at least two feet high and would give me all the height I needed. I climbed back up onto the table, grabbed the knife and another piece of cheese, carefully stepped up onto the bucket, and set to work on the screws.

It took all my strength to get them loose. Once started, though, it was a matter of patience. The knife slipped several times and I sliced my fingertip twice. Eventually though, I was working the last of the four screws loose.

Careful not to let the grate fall and crash against the table, I maneuvered the last screw out while bracing the grate with my head, then quickly grabbed it with my hands as it started to fall from its place.

I wobbled on my bucket and for a moment thought I was going to fall. But I recovered, took a deep breath, and stepped down. The square metal grate was four feet wide, so I needed both hands to set it aside. I was sweating when I climbed back up onto the bucket and poked my head through the hole.

It led to what looked like a square ventilation duct. Two feet in diameter, small, but I could fit. It ran straight in only one direction. I wasn't sure how far because the light was too dim. I wondered why this system would be in a house and thought maybe it had something to do with Mr. Pruitt's father's woodworking. That didn't matter. What did was where it came out.

What if it led me right back into the house? Then what would I do? It didn't matter. It was a risk I had to take. My fear roared, and I remembered the Great Teacher's love.

I can do this.

I climbed down and moved the tray Martha had brought away from the scene of the crime. I placed it by the door, grabbed the last piece of cheese, and stuffed the napkin in my back pocket. I didn't want anyone to connect Martha to helping me when they discovered I was gone.

Back up on the bucket I placed the knife inside the duct. With effort I hauled myself up into the small space. My shoulders brushed the walls and my head touched the top as I climbed inside. Knife in hand,

I army crawled down the shaft, trying to keep my movements light. I didn't want anyone to hear me and come looking. Martha had said something about it being late, so maybe the house was asleep. The light from my prison faded as I crawled and soon I was in total darkness.

I hoped I wouldn't run into any ten-inch worms. I shuddered and ignored the mental image playing at the back of my mind. The top of my head bumped into a hard surface and I knew the duct had ended. I reached out and felt empty space to my left, another hard surface to the right.

Left it was. I continued. A few minutes later I encountered another end and was forced right. The blackness seeming to get darker as I crawled. I prayed I wouldn't get stuck, and as if the Great Teacher heard me, a light ahead caught my eye. Another grate stood at the end of the long stretch. I felt the chill of air and knew the duct led outside!

I started moving faster, anxious to be out but cautious to remain stealthy. As I approached the end, I saw that a screen sealed off the duct to keep out critters and bugs. I used my knife to slice through the layers of screen and then pulled myself through.

The terminal grate stood another five feet or so on

the other side. I pulled myself close and saw that the screws on the outside had been loosened.

Martha.

She had risked all of this for me. I told myself I would never forget her kindness, and I prayed nothing came to harm her for it. I pushed the grate open and pulled myself out into the night air. I was along the back side of the mansion behind several rose bushes.

I replaced the grate and did my best to put the screws back in place but it was difficult in the darkness. Something snapped close by and I froze. To make it all this way and get caught! I held my breath and waited. It might have been an animal.

I yanked on the grate to make sure it was secure. *Good enough*, I thought.

I moved between the back of the house and the rose bushes. Most of the windows were dark. Once again I felt thankful for Martha. The large pine trees stood to the west. That was where Aggie had dug a way out under the fence. Would it still be there?

While I'd been locked inside, the snow had melted. Good—I wouldn't leave tracks this time. After drawing a deep breath, I ran. With all my might and without looking back, I tore across the property, the five pine trees in view. I was breathing heavily and shaking with nerves when I reached them.

I dropped to my knees to push away the piles of leaves. Relieved to see the hole hadn't been filled in, I crawled under the fence and then returned the leaves to hide the hole once more.

Facing the woods, I felt suddenly terrified. I didn't know the way.

Don't worry, Millie, I told myself. *You are never alone.* I closed my eyes and searched with my heart. It knew the way to the pool because it held the waters of the Great Teacher, and my heart knew him.

I felt the pull and didn't hesitate. Into the woods and through the trees. Across the bumpy ground, over the roots, and around the bushes. Toward the moon and the Great Teacher. I ran until I emerged from the trees into the sandy canyon with towering cliffs. My heart jumped with glee. I was close.

I found the boulder that hid the crack and worked my way inside, not fearing the darkness this time, for I knew where it was taking me. Within minutes I stood in the room with the pool. It was dark, the torches extinguished, but I could see the water's glow.

I walked to the edge, my whole body ready to follow the light.

"You found your way back," a voice said.

The torches ignited and the cave filled with light. Aggie stood beneath them. I squealed with shock that quickly turned to joy.

"Aggie!" I rushed to her. Her arms were extended for me and she chuckled as I fell into her embrace.

"It is good to see you too, child," Aggie said.

I pulled back from her warm hug. "I have so much to tell you," I said.

"Not now, you still have much to do," Aggie said.

"Wait. You said *found your way back*. Did you know I was here? Have you been waiting here this whole time? And why did I return to the attic and not this cave?"

"So many questions at once," Aggie teased.

I smiled, a tad embarrassed. "Did you know I had come back?"

"Yes."

"You didn't come for me."

"No, you needed to do this part of your journey on your own," Aggie said. "Well, not really on your own, because you're never alone."

I knew her meaning. "The Great Teacher is always with me."

She smiled broadly. "I never doubted you would find your way back." She kissed the top of my head and warmth filled me to my toes.

"Now you must go and finish what he has called you to," she said.

I waded into the pool a few feet. I turned back to Aggie.

"Will you watch over Martha for me?" I asked.

"Of course, I will keep a close eye on her."

Reassured, I continued into the water. When the water was over my head and shoulders, I dove toward the light. It surrounded me, pulled me in, and filled me with confidence. I was ready for whatever came next.

Chapter Nineteen

I woke up wet beside a pool. It was dark and cold and my mind tried to calculate where I was. What had happened? I remembered being in a beautiful golden field with Rebecca and the Great Teacher. Before that, eating worm sludge and being crippled with fear.

I pushed myself up and stared at the brilliant-blue pool. How did I get here? Had I been through the pool? Was I still at FIGS? As I searched for my memories, I rushed out of the cave and emerged onto the red dirt of the Shadowlands. Relief! I was still in the world of FIGS, but I had gone somewhere.

Or maybe I had come back from somewhere? I couldn't remember, but I knew diving through the pool altered memory. Wherever I had been, I didn't know what happened there. I did, however, remember FIGS, the Initiation, the school, my friends, my enemies, the dungeons, the marsh, the worm sludge.

A few memories felt a bit foggy, as though select moments at FIGS had been removed. But most of it was intact.

I shook my head and returned to what I knew for certain. In the golden field I had learned something incredible from the Great Teacher, and I needed to share it with the others. The sun was rising behind me. It was the third day of the Trial of Shadows and if we didn't get the golden vial before sunset we'd fail.

Unless I'd been gone too long. What if the others had gone on without me and I was here in the Shadowlands alone? Had I caused the group to fail because I left? I had to get back.

How I had reached the cave at the base of Shadow Mountain wasn't clear, but I knew the group had been digging for worm sludge just west of where we exited the marsh. I ran in that direction, hoping to find them there. The marsh lay to my left, Shadow Mountain to my right, and the sun rose at my back.

About five minutes later I stumbled across camp and felt a wave of relief. It was still there, the mats laid out and empty, the firepit smoking. I couldn't have been gone long.

Everyone must still be at the dig site.

Thirty yards ahead I found them huddled around a large hole.

Completely silent and kneeling on the ground with their backs to me, they dug frantically in the dirt. Dozens of holes covered the ground, making the earth uneven. I stared, afraid to approach.

I could hardly see their faces as they reached into the dirt and shoved their fingers into their mouths, licking them clean and going back for more. Like a pack of feasting hyenas. I took tentative steps toward the group and saw the back of Mac's head, her red hair matted with soil and twigs.

"Mac," I said. She didn't respond. She didn't even flinch. Worry blossomed in my gut.

"Polly," I said to the girl beside Mac. Again, nothing. They were like zombies, singleminded and ravenous.

What if I was too late?

I spotted Doris with them at the edge of the circle. She'd led them before. Maybe if I could get through to her she could lead them now. Maneuvering around a few holes but careful to keep my distance, I moved toward Doris.

"Doris," I said.

The girl stopped digging, raised her head from the hole, and turned to look at me. Her eyes were bloodshot, the skin underneath swollen and black. She said nothing and I inched back as she stared at me.

She opened her mouth and a deep growl rolled out. Terror gripped me. If I didn't get out of there, I'd be in deep trouble. I backed away and watched Doris turn her attention back to the hole. As soon as I had cleared the other holes, I started to run.

I fled toward Shadow Mountain, my mind searching for a solution. I stopped at the base of a foothill, my breathing heavy and my heart afraid. There was no way I could get them away from the dig site and up the mountain. But if we didn't get the vial we were all doomed.

Something chirped in a nearby tree, and I glanced up to see the blue bird I loved perched on a low branch. Paxaro. He leaped off his resting place, flew a couple yards ahead, and landed on the red dirt. He sang again and looked at me.

"What are you doing here?" I asked.

He responded by hopping toward Shadow Mountain. I followed him around a boulder, and there I saw a narrow twisting path leading up the mountainside. I followed it with my eyes until it disappeared into the dark shadows of the rocky cliffs.

I realized what the bird was suggesting. I had to go

get the golden vial myself. It was the only way to save my friends. But I couldn't possibly make the journey alone. And Dean Kyra said only the pure of heart could retrieve the vial.

What if that wasn't me? What if I couldn't do it?

I had eaten worm sludge. I couldn't be pure of heart.

Don't be afraid, for I am always with you, daughter.

The voice of the Great Teacher swirled through me and calmed my mounting fears. I wasn't alone, and the vial had to be retrieved. It was up to me.

"That's the way, huh?" I asked sheepishly.

Paxaro tweeted and took to the sky. He flew ten paces ahead and landed on the path's rocky edge, waiting for me to follow. I swallowed my fear and started.

CHAPTER TWENTY

The incline was steep, charging upward quickly and without mercy.

The sweet blue bird flew ahead, the only spot of color among the dark grays of the mountain's face. The sun continued to climb but offered no warmth. It was as if Shadow Mountain was separate from the rest of the Shadowlands. As if it existed in its own bitter-cold climate.

I shivered and hugged my arms to my chest. I was still damp from the pool and the cruel wind whipped across my clothes. Behind me the base of the mountain was no longer in sight. I could see the entire marsh, red dirt surrounding it as far as the eye could see.

The path seemed endless as it continued to climb into the low clouds. The steep, rocky mountainside rose on my left, while sharp cliffs dropped off along the right. One wrong step and . . .

Fear rooted me to the spot, but I knew I couldn't stop moving. I had to get the golden vial. Paxaro chirped above me and I was thankful for his company. One step after another. Hours passed, and the sun moved to the middle of the sky. It looked hot and bright, though I couldn't feel its warmth.

It started to snow, but only on the mountain. From this high up I could see that the rest of the Shadowlands were dry. I exhaled, my breath coming out in thin cloudy puffs. I wanted to stop, to go back, to surrender the idea that I could do this.

I am always with you.

I will never forsake you.

The Great Teacher's voice whispered in my heart. I could feel him through the cold, giving me strength.

Paxaro chirped loudly and landed inside a small nook at my eye level in the mountain's rocky face. The bird sang again and I knew he wanted me to come.

I walked to the hole and saw that a small brown sack had been stuffed inside at the back. It was tied up with thick red rope, and I had to stand on my tiptoes to yank it free. A simple white tag was attached to the red rope.

"Daughter," I said, reading the label out loud. The Great Teacher was the only one to ever call me that.

Paxaro tweeted happily and landed beside the sack. I quickly untied the rope and opened the bag. Reaching inside, my fingers found soft wool. I pulled the contents free. I stood and shook the garment out. It was a beautiful red cloak with delicate gold stitching along the edges and a heavy fur-lined hood.

Was it meant for me? And how had it gotten here?

I cover you in my love and will never forsake you.

My heart leaped with joy. Had the Great Teacher sent this for me? But even as I was asking the question, I knew the answer was yes. Excited, I placed the cloak over my shoulders and pulled the hood up. I'd never felt warmer. The cloak affirmed what I already knew.

The Great Teacher loved me.

He would always protect me, and I was never alone.

My strength was rejuvenated and I continued, quicker than before, with more determination and vigor. The cloak shielded me from the heavy snow and harsh wind as I moved up through the clouds.

When I broke through, the snow eased up and the wind died down. Five yards ahead, the narrow path led into a massive cave and I knew I'd arrived at the top of Shadow Mountain. Paxaro landed at the cave's wide mouth and I ran to keep up as the bird chirped wildly. I was almost there.

The cutout in the peak stood fifteen feet wide and

twice as high. When I stepped inside, torches came to life along the walls every four yards or so. They rested in iron sconces that jutted from the stone. They lit the path as I gazed deeper into the cave.

Paxaro stayed at the opening and I knew the rest of the journey was mine to take alone. I was suddenly afraid.

I turned to the small bird. "What if I'm not pure of heart?" I asked. "What if I fail?"

Paxaro cocked his head from side to side and then tweeted, soft and sweet.

I wished Rebecca were there to interpret. I breathed through my uncertainty. I had come this far and couldn't give up now. Paxaro let out a final chirp and took to the sky. I watched him go and then turned to face the cave.

The path was straight and wide as it pushed into the mountain. After a while I could no longer see the entrance. Behind me were only rocks and torches. I must have walked another hundred yards before stepping into a large room.

It was round like an atrium, and there were no torches here. Skylight from somewhere high above shined down and illuminated a stone table in the center of the space. A simple gold box sat on top.

I walked to the table and ran my fingers over the metal box. It was smooth and cool to the touch. It had no lock, no riddle. It was just a box. I popped open the top. A heart-shaped vial the size of my hand lay inside with a simple wooden crown etched onto its surface. The same crown was etched onto my medallion. It was beautiful.

The heart was filled with a shimmering white powder and was sealed with a cork. I wondered what it was for. I slowly reached into the box and lifted the vial, weighty in my hands. Power rumbled through my arms.

I couldn't believe it! I had gotten the golden vial. I could save my friends. We could complete the Trial of Shadows and go back to FIGS.

Chapter Twenty-One

I rushed down the cave path, running as fast as my legs could carry me. Once out, I was careful not to slip on the cold ground as I started downhill. I held the heart-shaped vial close to my chest, unwilling to risk anything happening to it.

Paxaro must have gone. The red cloak kept me warm as the wind whipped against my cheeks. I could hardly contain my excitement. We'd done it! I couldn't wait to get back to FIGS and have my friends return to normal.

It had taken me hours to climb the path but getting down was faster. Maybe it was the adrenaline. Maybe it was because I knew the way. Time flew, and before I knew it I was back on level ground.

Out of breath but too thrilled to stop, I traversed the

red dirt, heading toward the dig site. As I approached, I heard the screaming. Dread dropped into my stomach and I hurried. Once again the scene had shifted.

The other FIGS students were attacking each other like a pack of wild animals. Dash had Adam pinned against a tree and was screaming into his face about stealing sludge.

Polly sat on top of Lianna. The smaller girl cried for help.

Boomer and Mac shoved each other over a hole only big enough for one of them.

Others were pulling hair, clawing, screaming, demanding to know who had made the worms leave. Some wept, racked with loss. Others licked the dirt, desperate for more sweet slime.

"Millie!" someone shouted. Doris rushed to me, her face tortured. "Did you find more?"

"More?" I questioned.

"More worm goop," she said, frantic. "Isn't that why you left? To find more?"

They had run out.

"No, I didn't—"

"Ahhh!" She gripped the sides of her head. "This can't be happening!"

"Doris, it's okay," I said. "Look, I found the golden vial." I pulled the item from my cloak and held it out.

She dropped her hands and her expression soured. "You what?"

"I found the golden vial. That's why we're here. I did it!"

Others saw the vial and it drew their attention.

"Did you even go looking for worm sludge?" Doris demanded.

I was stunned. She didn't seem to care at all that I had succeeded.

"No, Doris. I got the vial so that we can complete the trial," I said.

"Lies," Doris hissed. "Only the pure of heart can get it, and everyone knows that isn't you."

"Doris—"

"It's a fake. You're trying to trick us! You're trying to get us to leave!" Doris yelled. The others drew close. Mac and Boomer stood at the back, their eyes bloodshot and faces pale.

"Please listen to me!" I appealed to the group. "I went up Shadow Mountain and found the golden vial. The Great Teacher led me there."

"So special," Doris teased. "Misfit Millie saves the day again."

My frustration grew. "Doris, you aren't thinking clearly."

"I'm thinking more clearly than I ever have! You

just can't stand it unless everyone's paying attention to you. Guess what? Nobody cares about your stupid vial."

Most of the faces bore dull expressions. They were so far gone! Doris was right. They didn't care.

"Give me the vial, Millie," Doris said.

"No."

With dark rage in her bloodshot eyes, Doris launched at me. She was so fast I couldn't react. She collided with me, nails out, and knocked me to the ground. My head slammed hard into the dirt. I tucked the vial into my chest to protect it.

She wrapped her fingers around mine and tried to yank it away.

"Give it to me!" she screamed.

The shoulder of my cloak ripped and my heart raged. The Great Teacher had given this to me and she was destroying it!

"Stop!" I yelled back. She was insane! She had done this. She had brought all the others here and hooked them on goop. She'd made them all rotten, and now they couldn't see the truth. She had destroyed my friends.

My fury rose like a serpent ready to strike. "Get off me!" I slammed my knee into her stomach, trying to hurt her as she hurt me.

Chapter Twenty-One

"Give it to me, you wretch!" Doris screamed.

"Never!"

Doris drew her hand back over her head and then brought her nails down across my cheek. She broke my skin. Pain erupted through my face and I cried out, the shock causing me to loosen my grip on the vial. She yanked it away. I brought my hand to my cheek and felt warm blood pooling under my palm.

Doris pushed off me and stood, the vial raised over her head. I scrambled to stand.

"Well, well," Doris started. "Looks like Misfit Millie isn't so powerful after all."

"Doris . . ." I tried. My cheek throbbed and blood trickled down my chin.

"Shut up!" she yelled. "I've had enough of you. We've all had enough of you and your 'I'm the chosen one' speech. You're just a weak, stupid little girl. And I hate you."

Doris threw the vial against a boulder. It smashed against the stone and shattered into hundreds of pieces.

"No!" I rushed to the broken glass.

"See," Doris said. "If you were pure of heart, if you were really chosen, this wouldn't have happened. But you're nothing, Millie Maven."

I stared at the broken vial. Tears stung my eyes and

I dropped to my knees. Doris had destroyed the only way to complete the trial and save my friends. I sniffed, collecting the larger pieces in my bloody palm. She had destroyed everything.

I hated her too.

A sweet fragrance filled my nostrils and invaded my senses. A deep powerful feeling buzzed under my skin. Somewhere in my angry sorrow Rebecca's words floated through: *Doris copes by hating anything she views as better than her, because she feels so inadequate.*

My heart exploded with the warmth of the Great Teacher as if I were back in the field of gold lying in his presence. His words sang over me and my anger started to fade.

I am in all. All are created in my image.

As you do unto others you do unto me.

Bless those who come against you, because they've only forgotten that they're perfectly loved. Show them, Millie. Show them my love.

How easy it was to forget the Great Teacher's truth. I looked up at Doris, who was mocking my tears, but I didn't care. Instead I was thinking about how much pain was in her heart. How much hurt she felt. How often she second-guessed her worth. I was seeing her clearly for the first time.

She and I were the same. Both full of fear and desperately trying to be good enough. I looked around at the others, who had been fighting one another for a bit of sludge. Sludge made them feel powerful, and they all felt powerless at times.

We were all the same. All created in one image. All perfectly loved. I was overcome with the realization and felt nothing but deep love for each of them.

Love them as I love them, Millie. That is your calling. It's why you were chosen.

But the vial was shattered.

Breathe in my love, daughter.

I looked down at the white powder that littered the ground and covered the boulder. The wind picked it up and swept it through the air. Immediately the light sweet scent filled me with wonder.

The vial held the power of love. I was breathing in love. And only love would save them, just as Rebecca had said.

Chapter Twenty-Two

Doris dropped to a squat in front of me and grabbed a piece of glass. "Sad, sad little Misfit," she teased.

"I'm sorry, Doris," I said. "I'm sorry you feel worthless, but you're not. You're beautiful and perfectly loved."

She looked like I'd reached out and slapped her. She opened her mouth but nothing came out.

"I'm afraid too," I continued. "I feel like I'm never enough, but then I remember what the Great Teacher says about me. That I am loved and chosen and his. He says the same thing about you, Doris. He loves you too."

Tears filled her eyes. She stood and stepped back from me as if I'd become a monster she feared. I stood, still holding her eyes.

"It's okay. We don't have to be afraid," I said. "We just forget sometimes how loved we are. But I'm learning to remember. I can help you learn too." I felt the love rise up around me. Just as the marsh air had contained power to bring out our fears, the contents of the vial held the power to return us to love.

We just had to breathe it in. It wouldn't take long for it to reach everyone. Doris would be the first. I could see it working as she inhaled. Her eyes started to change.

The red blood vessels in her eyes shrank and then disappeared. She stumbled backward and she gasped. A shiver ran through her body. I untied the nape of my cloak and offered it to her. She hesitantly took it and wrapped it around her shoulders.

The same thing started to happen to those closest to her, which drew the curiosity of those farther back. Everyone drew closer.

Polly and Lianna and Adam. As they breathed, their eyes cleared and their dark circles lost their tint. Dash and Mac were next. Then Boomer. I watched as the love that floated in the air washed over him.

Tears of joy filled my eyes and I rushed for the boy. I wrapped my arms around his neck and pulled him close.

"Boomer," I cried.

"I . . . I . . ." He could only stutter, but he didn't need to say anything.

"I love you, friend. I love you," I said.

He hugged me back, his warm tears soaking the shoulder of my shirt. When I pulled back, Boomer's cheeks were wet with tears. "I'm so sorry—"

"It's okay," I said. "You just forgot who you were. I forgive you."

"Millie," a soft voice said behind me. I turned to see Mac, eyes tearful and sheepish.

"Mac!" I pulled her close.

"You saved us," Mac said.

"It wasn't me. It was the Great Teacher."

"I can feel his love," she said softly.

"Me too," Boomer added.

I held their hands and smiled. No other words were needed.

Everyone slowly came back from their fogged state and remembered what they had said or done. Their guilt and sadness were heavy. But a strong sense of love that hung in the air gave us all hope. Many cried together, apologized, tried to make sense of what had happened. Many said, "I love you." Many held each other.

I looked for Doris, who was reuniting with her brother, my red cloak still wrapped around her shoulders. She must have felt me watching because she turned to look at me. I held her eyes, sent her love from where I stood, and sensed she wasn't ready to receive it.

She dropped her gaze and turned back to her brother. It didn't bother me. Loving her wasn't about her loving me back. It was just about loving her.

Rebecca and Dean Kyra had said the Shadowlands would bring out our fear and darkness to divide us. But the love of the Great Teacher had now united us.

We knew the truth. We were one.

An hour passed as our tears turned to laughter. The sun started to set and we talked about getting firewood. I wasn't sure what would happen next. We'd retrieved the golden vial, but we'd also broken it. We may have failed the Trial of Shadows after all. Maybe, when the sun finally faded behind the mountains, we would all be sent back to our homes outside the world of FIGS. No one knew.

But as we waited, we continued to bond. We were different from when we'd started, as if nothing could separate us. I sat between Mac and Boomer and told them of my adventure up the mountain.

Suddenly the back of my medallion grew hot against my chest. I yelped and lifted it away from my skin.

"What?" Mac asked.

"My medallion is burning," I said, turning it over.

Mac leaned in and gasped, as did Boomer.

"Whoa," Boomer said.

A new image had formed on the back. It was etched into the metal, just like the crown on the front, except it was a golden heart.

"What are you guys looking at?" Polly walked over.

"Come look!" Mac yelled to the whole group. "Her medallion changed!"

Students scurried over, everyone wanting to get a look at the new image. I pulled the medallion off my neck so people could get a better view. My mind tumbled over why it had happened and what it meant.

"I bet it's because you were the one who got the golden vial," Adam said.

"Makes sense," Polly added.

I didn't know, but I was sure to ask Dean Kyra when we got back to FIGS.

As if responding to my thoughts, the ground shook. A straight, illuminated path rose from the marsh. We scrambled to our feet as we watched the path until it stopped rising.

"Another challenge?" Dash asked.

"No," I thought out loud. "A way back to FIGS."

We had completed the Trial of Shadows.

CHAPTER TWENTY-THREE

W̲e followed the path through the marsh all day to its very end beyond the wetlands. We saw no dungeons this time, only Dean Kyra and the professors, who watched us approach as the sun sank behind the distant mountains.

"We made it," Mac breathed beside me.

"Just in time," Boomer added. "I'm starved."

Dean Kyra studied us all with curious eyes, then she stepped up to me and examined my medallion, turning it over. The new golden heart gleamed bright.

Her eyes lifted to meet mine and she offered me a nod. "Well done." She stepped away and addressed us all. "Well done, all of you! We'll celebrate your victory, but first you should rest. What you faced over the last few days was no small challenge. Come."

She turned and with a wave of her hand caused a door to appear from thin air. I blinked, still surprised by the wonder of FIGS. One by one we entered a stone passageway that took us back into the main entryway of FarPointe Institute, and we gathered there just as we had on our first day. As soon as we were all through, the door vanished.

Just like that, the Shadowlands were gone.

The sun was still in the sky at FIGS, even though it had set in the Shadowlands. Bright light poured through the windows and warmed the front room. Those of us with wounds were healed by Professor Gabriel, who moved around the room using his gift. I'd nearly forgotten the large cut that ran along my face until he laid his palm on my cheek. Warmth spread over my face. When he withdrew his hand, I lifted my fingers to feel new, smooth skin. Amazing.

I glanced at Doris, who was watching me. She dropped her eyes and I knew she was still dealing with guilt. Professor Claudia directed us to our rooms for much-needed rest and no one had to be told twice. Everyone was exhausted.

"Here," someone said as I started up the stairs. I turned to see Doris holding out my red cloak.

"You can keep it if you'd like," I offered.

"No, you should have it," Doris said. Her voice was

thin and tired, but not unkind. I could see pain and uncertainty in her eyes. She had felt the love of the Great Teacher, but she was resisting it like I had at first.

I smiled and took the cloak, knowing I was called to continue to offer her love even if she rejected it. She walked past me up the stairs and I returned my gaze to the soft wool cloak in my hand. It was dirty and ripped. The gold embroidered edge was tattered but that made it even more beautiful. It told a story now.

"Where did you get that?"

I looked up to see Professors Alexandria and Gabriel standing on the steps above me, staring at my cloak. Dean Kyra stood within earshot, watching curiously.

"The Great Teacher gave it to me on the mountain," I said.

"You saw him?" Professor Gabriel asked.

"No. Paxaro led me to it. He's Rebecca's bird." I chuckled. "He named himself."

"A bird?" Professor Alexandria asked sharply.

"A very special bird," I said.

"And how do you know the cloak was meant for you?" the grumpy teacher asked.

I thought back to the tag bearing the word "daughter" and smiled.

"It had my name on it," I said.

Professor Alexandria huffed and shook her head. "Why would the Great Teacher give you such a gift?"

My first instinct was to say that it shielded me from the cold but I knew it was more than that. I locked eyes with Professor Alexandria and answered without doubt. "Because he loves me."

Her eyes widened slightly before softening. I wondered if she knew how much the Great Teacher loved her.

A moment later her face returned to the normal stern state I was used to, and she extended her hand. "It's filthy," she said. "I'll have it mended and cleaned for you."

I gave her the cloak. "Cleaned but not mended, if you don't mind. I like it the way it is."

She held it carefully and scoffed at me. "You should show more respect for something so precious." Then she turned and strode across the entry room, out of sight.

I looked at Professor Gabriel, who chuckled and gave me a kind wink. "Go rest, Millie Maven."

I had questions. Why had the worm sludge affected me differently than it had the others? And why had I gone through a pool? For that matter, what had happened when I did? I could only remember my encounter with Rebecca and the Great Teacher, though I had a feeling there was more.

But I was too tired for questions right now. I nodded and continued back up the stairs.

Inside my dorm room, I went straight to my bed, grateful for sheets and blankets and pillows and sleep. I was dirty and knew I should shower first, but I was too tired. I fell asleep quickly.

CHAPTER TWENTY-FOUR

When I awoke a few hours later the room was empty.

I sat up and heard the soft melody of music drifting under the door. The celebration had started! I jumped up and rushed through a shower, put on fresh clothes, and brushed my hair. I was about to leave when I noticed the small white journal Dean Kyra had given me my first day inside FIGS. The Great Teacher's journal.

I picked it up and ran my fingers across the sword on the front. It tingled under my skin as I cracked open the cover. The pages were still blank. All of them. But I could feel the power of the book and knew there was something there. I just couldn't see it yet. Its meaning would come to me when I needed it most, just like the red cloak.

I tucked the journal back inside my wardrobe chest and left the room. It was dark outside, and the moon filtered in through the tall glass windows as I rounded the corner toward the staircase.

The music was coming from the dining hall. I descended the wide staircase and had turned to head toward the party when a muffled voice pulled my attention. I stopped. The sound was coming from opposite the dining hall, near the library.

I slowly walked toward it. The large double doors stood propped open. I glanced through and saw someone standing in the dimly lit hallway, in front of the locked door that opened to the dungeons.

It was Doris. My heart spiked as I listened to her whispers. Was she talking to herself? No, not Doris. She was up to something and I doubted it was good.

I stepped into the hallway. "Doris?"

She snapped her head toward me and quickly slid something into her pocket.

"What are you doing?" I asked suspiciously.

"Are you checking up on me?" she snapped.

"No," I said. "I was headed for the party and heard you talking."

She walked down the hallway toward me. "And you saw it was me and assumed I was up to no good. I know what you think of me." Her words weren't mean, only hurt. And she was right. I had assumed the worst.

Rebecca's words returned to me. *You are not called to judge her. You are called to love her.* I had forgotten so quickly.

"I was talking through my *feelings*," Doris said, making air quotes with her fingers. "Professor Alexandria suggested I try it and I didn't want anyone to hear me."

"I'm sorry, Doris," I said. "I shouldn't have judged you."

"That's what we do, judge each other," Doris said.

"We could stop. We could try to be friends."

She stared at me for a long, quiet moment. Then she dropped her eyes and shook her head. "We can't be friends, Millie. That's just not who we are."

"Doris—"

"And I don't want to be friends," she said, her eyes coming back up to meet mine. "Okay?"

Bless those who come against you, because they've only forgotten they are perfectly loved. Love her, Millie.

I nodded. "Okay."

"Please leave me alone," Doris said as she brushed by me.

I didn't want to leave her, and my gut was still telling me something else was going on, but I did what she asked and turned toward the party.

Love her, I heard again.

I would. I knew she was on a journey to remembering the truth, just like I was. I would try not to judge her journey and instead offer her the love of the Great Teacher often.

I crossed the main entry and entered the dining hall. Joyful music and laughter swept over me as I pushed through the doors. Everyone was gathered at the tables, eating a feast fit for kings.

Mac waved me over. I chased all ideas of Doris away and rushed to sit with my friends. We feasted and laughed and sang as the professors' band entertained us with their happy tunes.

I noticed Doris join a little while later and smiled at her. She looked away, set in her old habits once again. Honestly, I felt sorry for her.

Lianna pulled Mac and me from where we sat and spun us around as we danced across the floor. Boomer and Harvey were doing the robot, which didn't match the music at all. Adam and Dash were laughing and couldn't help but join in. Before we knew it, Professor Claudia had jumped in the middle and was doing her own robot moves. We applauded and cheered for the sweet teacher and soon everyone was dancing.

The night grew late and I left the floor, laughing and

searching for water. Dean Kyra stood at the beverage table and smiled at me as I approached.

"Enjoying yourself?" Dean Kyra asked.

"Yeah, this is awesomesauce," I said, using Mac's term.

Dean Kyra chuckled. "Awesomesauce indeed."

I drank my water, the cold liquid giving relief to my dry throat.

"Dean Kyra?" I asked after a couple moments of silence.

"Yes, Miss Maven," she said.

"Why did the worm sludge affect me differently than the others?"

"I can't be certain, but I would guess it has something to do with your connection to the Great Teacher," she said.

"How so?"

"Your path is unique, Millie. I would say the Great Teacher has something special in mind for you. Your journey won't always look like the others.'"

"Is that why I went back through the pool?'

She turned and looked at me, surprised. "You went through a pool? While in the Shadowlands?"

"Yes. I mean, I think so." I told her about being full of fear and rushing away from the digging. I told her about the field and then waking up beside a pool, wet, having lost time. "Also my medallion," I said. "It changed."

"Indeed. May I see it again?"

I pulled the medallion off and handed it to her. She rubbed her thumb over the back where the heart was etched. "I haven't seen this symbol in some time."

"What does it mean?" I asked.

"It signifies a pure heart, free of judgment. Usually the entire group has to work together to retrieve the vial, but you managed alone. My guess is that whatever the Great Teacher showed you in that field prepared you." She paused and smiled. "And maybe you wouldn't have ended up in that field if you hadn't traveled back through the pool. The Great Teacher is getting you ready for something remarkable."

Something about her words made me think of Doris standing in front of the dungeon door. I glanced up to see that she was watching me from across the room. Things between us weren't over.

"I'm afraid I won't be strong enough," I said.

"We're never given anything we can't handle, Miss Maven. If the Great Teacher called you to this path, you will be ready," she said.

I wished I had as much confidence in myself as she did. I glanced back to Doris, but she was gone.

"Something significant is coming," Dean Kyra said, her voice now somber. "I can feel it too." Then she placed her hand on my shoulder and gave a soft squeeze. "But not tonight."

She walked back to the center of the room, clapped her hands twice, and waited for the room to fall silent.

"Well done, students of FIGS. You have successfully completed the Trial of Shadows!"

The room filled with applause and she continued when the clapping slowed.

"You have now seen one another in a new light. This new perception will aid you in what comes next. As your time at FIGS draws to a close, you will face your greatest challenge. This one will require you to distinguish truth from lies. For that, you will need one another."

I joined Mac on the outside of the group. She looped her arm through mine. I was so happy to have her back to normal. I didn't know what we would face next, but I knew I couldn't do it without her.

"Now that you have been down in the dungeons, you understand the dangers it holds. Sometimes students feel the urge to return. You must not go back there. We have sealed it for your own good, but over the years some students have broken the seal. So I offer you this warning. Whatever you do, you must not write in the book of history that may be found within the tunnels."

"Book of history?" Adam whispered.

"I didn't see a book, did you?" Polly asked Lianna. The two had become best friends even though Polly had bitten Lianna in the Shadowlands.

"She's talking about the book we saw in the locked cell, isn't she?" Mac whispered.

Yes, I thought.

"Do you hear me?" Dean Kyra continued. "Stay away from the book."

"Why? It's just a book," Boomer said.

Dean Kyra's brow arched. "No," she said. "It's far more dangerous than just any book. If even one among you breaks this rule, all will be lost. All will be destroyed. It only takes one Judas."

I felt a stare and saw Doris watching me again. Curiosity spiked, but I brushed it aside as Dean Kyra continued.

"All that you have faced has been for the transformation of your truest gift: your heart," Dean Kyra said. "The purpose of FIGS is for far more than to develop your physical gifts. It's about your hearts, because only a healed heart can heal the world from which you came."

She smiled and spread her arms wide. "But for now we continue to celebrate the unity you discovered through the love of the Great Teacher!"

Professor Gabriel started up his fiddle again and the music returned. We danced more, ate more, laughed more, until we were all so filled with happiness we could burst.

I even saw Doris smile once or twice. Yes, something was coming. Something darker than I had yet faced. But as Dean Kyra had said, not tonight. Tonight I would bask in the Great Teacher's perfect love for me and for all.

It was stronger than any darkness coming.

What could stand against me if I stood in his perfect love?

His love would be my strength.

I just had to remember.

Dancing there with my friends, I tried to ignore the dread that started to open in my chest. *I just had to remember*, I told myself.

For the sake of everyone, I prayed I could.

EPILOGUE

Priscilla descended the stairs to the basement. Two days had passed since she'd locked Millie inside. Two days of searching for Aggie. Priscilla needed to know what the wretched old woman might have said to expose the truth about Millie's past. Priscilla doubted Aggie knew the whole story, but on the chance she did know something . . .

A chill snaked down her back. They couldn't have people snooping around! Too many questions might lead to answers that would destroy them. That rebellious little girl could ruin everything.

Her husband had left earlier that morning for a weeklong business trip to Singapore, and Priscilla knew she needed to whip Millie back into shape before Augustus returned.

She'd concocted many punishments to ensure the girl would never break the rules again. When Priscilla was finished, Millie would serve her like a lady-in-waiting.

She crossed the basement to the locked door, twisted her key in the lock, and popped the door open. Priscilla took in the room and froze. The ceiling grate rested on the table beside a large white upended bucket.

Reality crashed down on her. Dread filled her bones and anger rushed through her blood as she started screaming at the empty room.

Millie was gone.

TO BE CONTINUED

DON'T MISS THE EPIC FINALE
IN MILLIE MAVEN BOOK 3